THE FORSAKEN VAMPIRE

DIRTY BLOOD
BOOK 4

PENELOPE BARSETTI

HARTWICK PUBLISHING

Hartwick Publishing

The Forsaken Vampire

Copyright © 2023 by Penelope Barsetti

All rights reserved.

No part of this book may be reproduced in any form or by any electronic or mechanical means, including information storage and retrieval systems, without written permission from the author, except for the use of brief quotations in a book review.

CONTENTS

1. Harlow — 1
2. Harlow — 19
3. Aurelias — 45
4. Huntley — 49
5. Harlow — 59
6. Harlow — 83
7. Ivory — 89
8. Harlow — 103
9. Harlow — 117
10. Aurelias — 137
11. Huntley — 151
12. Huntley — 179
13. Ivory — 195
14. Harlow — 209
15. Aurelias — 229
16. Harlow — 237
17. Huntley — 255
18. Aurelias — 267
19. Harlow — 293
20. Huntley — 317
21. Ian — 321
22. Huntley — 341
23. Harlow — 361
24. Ivory — 371
25. Huntley — 377
26. Ivory — 385
27. Huntley — 391
28. Aurelias — 397

1

HARLOW

A vase of lilies sat in the center of the table, the long stems extending to beautiful white flowers on top. Condensation formed on the surface of the glass like the flowers had just been picked that morning. My eyes glazed over as I stared at the flowers in the center, listening to Atticus speak to Violet beside him.

"How's your family?" he asked, handsome in his buttoned coat and trousers.

"They're well," she said. "But Mother has been slowing down without my father around…"

"I'm sorry to hear that."

"My mother is pressuring me to marry. As an only child, I don't have a brother to head the household."

It took all my strength not to roll my eyes.

Atticus clearly didn't know what to say to that because he didn't say anything at all. The awkward silence stretched until Atticus turned his gaze to the same flowers I stared at.

I decided to jump in. "Want my advice, Violet?" I turned to look at her head-on. "Don't wait for a man to save you. Save yourself. Advice my mother gave me that I impart to you."

Violet seemed to take that as an insult because she silently excused herself from the table.

Atticus released a quiet sigh before he looked at me. "Why do you do that?"

"What?" The room was full of the stewards of the other Kingdoms, stewards who served King Rolfe—my father. It was a luncheon, the kind of social event that my father despised but my mother encouraged. According to her, there were other ways of earning loyalty besides demanding it.

"Don't what me, Harlow."

I rolled my eyes and looked away. "There's nothing less attractive than a desperate woman. Please tell me you're smart enough not to fall for that ploy."

"But you don't need to be rude."

"She was rude first."

"How?"

"Because she only wants you for something—since you're the future king. When a woman's affection for my brother is true, then I won't be rude." I looked away again, ignoring the food on my plate.

"We don't know if I'm the future king. You're the eldest."

"But I'm a woman."

"You know Father doesn't care about that."

"But he also knows I've got a mouth that breathes fire just like a dragon."

He cracked a smile even though he tried to hide it. "You're right about that."

The musicians stopped their song, and all the chatter in the hall died away. Our attention turned to the double doors that would soon open. I had to shift in my chair to see past the enormous vase that was too big for the table.

Then the trumpets started, and the servants opened both doors simultaneously, revealing my father in his king's uniform, his sword at his hip, even though he hadn't served in battle since before I was born. Tall, muscular, with eyes that could kill, he stared straight ahead with an attitude that clearly said, "I don't want to be here." He moved into the room, flanked by his guard, crossing the checkerboard tiles between the table as he approached the throne that waited for him.

As he drew close, his eyes shifted to the table where we sat.

I smiled, knowing how much he hated this diplomatic bullshit.

It was too subtle for anyone but me to notice, a smile in his eyes rather than on his lips. It lasted less than a second before his eyes were forward again. He reached the top of the rise, turned around and regarded all the stewards who served him, and then took a seat, the crown of jewels upon his head.

The room was full of sculptures by the best artists in the city, humanlike statues that captured beauty in solid rock. With glasses of wine in their hands, our parents drifted across the room and mingled with all the guests at the luncheon. My brother and I watched from our seats, trying not to laugh at the look of consternation on Father's face.

"He looks like he's in physical pain," Atticus said with a smirk. "You'd think he'd be used to this by now."

"Does anyone ever get used to bullshit?"

My brother looked at me. "You're the one in a pretty dress with flowers in your hair."

"Just because this is bullshit doesn't mean I can't look nice."

"Look." He nodded in their direction. "I don't think he's said a word this whole time."

"Mother is much better at this sort of thing." She was in a red gown with draped sleeves that exposed her shoulders. It was tight on her waist, her dark hair stretching down her back in beautiful curls. I looked just like my mother—but I had my father's soul.

"Are you going to tell Father about Ethan?"

I turned at the mention of his name. "How do you know about that?"

He rolled his eyes slightly. "It's not exactly a secret."

"Well, I haven't told anyone." Was Ethan blabbing about his conquests to everyone?

"So, you admit it?" My brother looked at me head on.

"Did you just set me up?" My eyes narrowed.

A slow smirk moved on to his lips.

"Bastard."

He gave a quiet chuckle.

"I can't believe Ethan is talking."

"He's not. He's *showing*."

Now my eyebrows furrowed in confusion.

He looked past me and nodded toward a sculpture on the other side of the room. It was of a beautiful woman with a flower crown upon her head, one strap of her dress dropped to expose a single, perky breast. Even in stone, her expression was distinctive, and it didn't take more than a glance to see the similarities.

Heat flushed my cheeks in embarrassment because it was so obvious.

"You're lucky Mother and Father don't care for the art they commissioned."

Ethan's balls were going to meet my heel next time we spoke.

"Seems serious."

"We aren't talking about this."

"Oh, but you can stick your nose in between me and Violet?"

"Are you sleeping with her?"

"No—"

"Then it's not the same thing," I said. "Please don't tell Mother and Father."

Atticus stared at me, an eyebrow raised.

"And don't use it as blackmail either."

"I didn't realize you had such a low opinion of me."

"You're the one who hid rotten eggs in my bedroom because you were mad at me."

"I was twelve."

"Whatever. I still can't get that smell out of my nose ten years later."

A smile cracked his lips. "Your secret is safe with me, Harlow. So…is it serious?"

I didn't have to think twice about my answer. "No."

"Well, he seems to think it is."

"I wouldn't interpret the depth of his feelings based on a statue."

"It's not a statue. It's a declaration of love."

"We aren't even sure if that statue is based on me—"

"Come on, Harlow." He eyed me.

"Drop it," I said in a whisper. "They're coming." We both rose to our feet to greet our parents.

Mother came to me first, her hands moving to my forearms to give me an affectionate squeeze. "I love those flowers." She admired the white flowers woven into the crown made of branches.

"Thank you," I said. "But you're the one who's a hot piece of ass."

She burst into a laugh as she dropped her hands.

"You're fire, Mother." I looked her up and down. "That dress…"

Her laugh subsided into a grin. "Thank you, honey." She brought me into a hug and kissed my temple.

Father came to me after he embraced Atticus.

"Doesn't she look hot?" I asked.

A subtle grin was on his lips, but his eyes stayed on me. "Atticus tells me you chased off Violet."

"That's an exaggeration." I wasn't too annoyed, because I'd rather talk about Violet than my secret lover. Mother drifted to Atticus and smothered him in the same affection. "I just told her to take care of herself instead of expecting someone else to do it."

"That would be fine advice if it weren't coming from a place of privilege, Harlow."

"I'm not coming from a place of privilege," I said. "My father had to overthrow the barbarians who took what didn't belong to them, and he and my mother had to defeat Necrosis to save everyone on the continent. You had to work your ass off for that crown—and that blood of survival runs in my veins."

He stared with his crystal-blue eyes that reminded me of a frozen lake in winter. His thoughts were bottled deep inside, and the only person who could read his expression was my mother. But the seconds ticked by, and then the light returned to his eyes. "You're so much like your mother."

"Really?" I said. "Because she says I'm just like you."

A subtle smile moved on to his lips as his arm circled my shoulder. He brought me in close and pressed a kiss to my temple before he let me go. "I have a meeting with the stewards. Stay out of trouble."

"When have I ever been in trouble?"

The corner of his mouth cocked in a smile before he walked off.

I left the castle after dark and walked the cobblestone streets until I reached the shop where Ethan worked. He lived directly above it on the second floor, but I knew he worked all hours, whenever inspiration hit him, so he was probably downstairs. The door was unlocked, so I walked inside and made my way past the front counter to the wide space in the rear. A partially completed statue stood in the center, piles of broken pieces of marble on the floor beneath. He stood on top of a table, so focused on the chiseling of the stone he didn't notice me. There were pencil marks where the cuts were supposed to happen, and he struck his tool and shaved off another piece.

It wasn't a naked woman, but a king with a crown upon his brow, his sword at his side. The face was blank at the moment, but I knew exactly who it was supposed to be. "There's no way my father asked for this."

Ethan stilled when he heard my voice, and then he glanced at me. He didn't let me interrupt him and finished the shoulder that he was carving. A minute of silence passed as more debris fell to the floor. Then he hopped off the table and tossed his tools aside. "Your mother did."

"I hope you aren't attached to it—because he'll destroy it."

He wiped his hands on a towel as he approached me, dust and paint on his clothes. "The best part of art is making it."

"I thought it was looking at it?"

"I enjoy looking at art—as long as it's not my own." He tossed the towel aside then came close, stopping just an inch from my face. His dark eyes looked into mine, shifting back and forth. "You have something to say to me?"

"How did you know?"

"Because I know you, Harlow." He stepped back without giving me a kiss. "What is it?"

"You thought no one would notice that statue you did yesterday?" My arms crossed over my chest.

"I hoped they'd notice."

"And what if my father noticed?"

Unapologetic, he just stared. "Art is about truth. And I won't lie—not even to him."

"Lie about what?"

He stared, his eyes hard.

"It's like you want to get caught."

"Maybe I do."

I stepped closer, my arms still crossed. "Well, you got your wish, because my brother figured it out pretty quickly. You know how awkward that was?"

"And what did you tell him?"

"I didn't have to tell him anything because the truth was too apparent."

His face remained stoic, but there was a flash of triumph in his eyes.

"Don't do that again."

"Don't tell me how to make my art."

"I'm not telling you how to make your art. I'm telling you not to use my image without my consent. You had my tit hanging out, for fuck's sake. If my father figured it out, you'd be dead right now, you know that?"

"King Rolfe is a fair ruler. The only people he's put to death are traitors."

"He'd make an exception for the man who put his daughter's body on display without her permission."

Now he crossed his arms over his chest. "I won't apologize for it."

"I'm not looking for an apology. Just don't do it again."

He stared at me.

I stared back.

"Is this fight over?"

Not for me. "What are you trying to do?"

"You need to be more specific than that."

"You made that statue for a reason."

"I'm an artist—"

"Bullshit." I walked up to him, like I might push him in the chest. "What's your endgame?"

He tilted his head slightly to look down at me. "It's been three months."

"Wow, you're good at math."

He ignored my sarcasm. "If this were a fling, it would be over by now. So that means it's a clandestine affair—and I don't want to be a secret anymore."

"You definitely aren't a secret with a statue like that."

"Harlow." His voice deepened in annoyance. "I know how smart you are. You knew this conversation was coming. You've known my feelings for a long time, and if you didn't, you know now."

My heart raced like the flapping wings of a frantic bird.

"I don't want to be a secret anymore."

"I'm the Princess of Delacroix."

"So?"

"I can't just marry anyone—"

"Your father would let you marry anyone you wanted, so that's a bullshit excuse."

My eyes shifted away because his stare was too much.

"Harlow."

I still wouldn't look at him.

"Come on."

I took a breath and looked at him again.

"What is it? I'm not good enough for you?"

"Please don't do this."

"Don't do what, Harlow?"

"*This*." My arms tightened over my chest. "You should have just left it alone."

Once the truth seeped into his pores, he hardened his stare in a new way.

"It was fun...easy. And now it's a *thing*. A thing we have to talk about. And I promise you, the more we talk, the worse it's going to get. So, let's just...stop."

He breathed in the silence, his hard expression slowly morphing into one of pain. "All this meant nothing to you?"

"That's not what I said."

"Then it meant something to you."

"Of course it did, Ethan."

"Then why am I getting dumped right now?"

"You wouldn't be getting dumped if you'd just left it alone."

"Why?" he pressed. "Why?"

I stayed quiet.

"Harlow."

"Just because I enjoy being with you now doesn't mean I want to be with you forever." It was a harsh thing to say after he'd basically told me he loved me, but it was the truth. "Just because you won't be my husband doesn't mean I wanted it to end yet. Not every relationship needs to end with a happily ever after. Most don't. But now that you're forcing this conversation…it has to end."

His expression hadn't changed at all. His face was still hard as stone. He didn't blink.

I felt like shit. "I'm sorry—"

"Because I'm an artist? Because I'm not rich?"

"No," I said. "I just don't love you."

2

HARLOW

I sat in the nook beneath my windowsill, flipping my dagger out of the sheath before flipping it back. Back and forth I went, not paying attention to my movements because it was second nature at this point. My four-poster bed was unmade because I hadn't left my quarters for the maids to clean. My sword leaned against the wall beside my bed. The curtains over the windows were champagne pink. My bedroom was in the corner of the castle, so I had a view of the village and the mountains in the distance.

A knock sounded on my door.

I continued to flip my dagger. "Yeah?"

The door opened, and my father appeared, dressed in his armor even though I'd never seen him ride into battle. His helmet was tucked under his arm. "Get dressed and grab your sword."

I'd forgotten it was Wednesday. "I'm kinda tired today…"

He stared down at me like he hadn't heard what I said.

I flipped my dagger back into the sheath.

His stare was still rock hard.

"We aren't at war or anything—"

"But we must be prepared for it. I won't ask again." He walked out and shut the door behind him.

I gave a sigh and got dressed.

My father and I had been training my entire life. I was so young when we started that I didn't actually remember when the training began. It was just something we'd always done, every Wednesday, the only exception when we'd all been bedridden with a terrible flu one winter.

My father was the best swordsman I'd ever seen. I watched him challenge multiple soldiers at once without getting a scratch on his armor. His core was always tight and his hits strong, so it was more of a dance than a battle.

I hoped to be as good as him one day, but I wasn't sure if that was possible.

We moved to the field underneath the shade of the trees and began our session. He no longer instructed me. All we did was spar, because experience was the best teacher. He came at me with his blade and was stopped by my block. He kept up his advance, trying to drive me back, but I struck him with a flurry of blows then rolled out of the way to get the upper hand.

"Attagirl." The better I did, the harder he pushed me, making me sweat so much my fingers became slippery on the hilt. Whenever I had a chance, I wiped my fingers on my leg just to dispel the moisture.

He took the opening to knock my sword out of my hand. "How many times have I told you to wear gloves?"

I rolled out of the way and grabbed my sword in the process, dodging his attacks with my speed. I kicked him in the shin then hit my sword hard down on his, forcing it toward the earth so I could punch him in the face.

His head turned with the blow, but it was back in a second, pride in his eyes. He came at me harder than ever before, moving with a speed I could barely challenge. It required me to be on the defensive because he was too powerful. He pushed me to the brink, forced me to ignore the stitch in my side and keep going. All I could do was block his hits as I frantically sought an opening to do some damage.

I caught his sword the way he taught me and forced it to spin, forced it to leave his fingers so it would fly across the field.

But he didn't stop to stare at me with pride. He came at me with his fists, grabbed me by the wrist to get the sword out of my hands.

I twisted out of his hold just the way he'd taught me and kicked him.

He continued to come at me, his hand flying for my neck because he never went easy on me, not even as his daughter.

I threw my elbow down on his arm and kicked him at the same time.

It was enough to make him falter back a few steps.

I sprinted, knowing this was the only opening I would get. I jumped on him and pushed the steel of my blade against his neck. I panted hard because I was fucking exhausted. My muscles screamed for respite.

He lay there with the sword against him, looking at me with unmistakable pride. Then a gentle smile moved on to his lips. "Attagirl."

I dropped my sword and sat on the grass, taking a moment to catch my breath.

He sat upright and rested his arms on his knees, facing the other way. "You're a better soldier than most of my men."

"Does that mean I'll fight in the next war? If there's another one."

"There will be another one. There always is. But no."

"No?" I asked in surprise. "Then why have you been training me since I could walk?"

"Because I won't always be around to protect you, Harlow."

My heart tightened as if squeezed by a fist. "Don't say things like that."

"And I don't want you to depend on a man for protection either."

"Well, I definitely don't."

"Always be prepared."

"Father, you're a revered king. You have no enemies."

"Your enemies won't make themselves known until the most opportune time for them." He stared across the distance, his warm pride gone and replaced by a callous coldness. "And the best way to gain my cooperation is through you and Atticus. You must always be prepared."

I knew my father was paranoid for a reason. His father had been murdered and his mother raped right before his eyes. Everything that belonged to his family was taken away—because they hadn't expected it. "Well, no one can touch me. You've seen to that, Father."

"I hope so, sweetheart."

I sat at my vanity and wiped the makeup from my face with the warm towel the maids brought when they provided turn-down service. Then I brushed my long hair, gently getting the tangles out. Quiet moments like these were the hardest, because I was suffocated by my own thoughts, by the pain in my heart.

Knock. Knock. Knock. The gentle tapping struck my door.

"Come in."

The door opened, and I could see my mother's reflection in my mirror. Makeup was gone from her face too, and she wore her robe over her nightdress. Her long hair was down over one shoulder, and seeing both of our reflections in the mirror reminded me of the similarities in our appearances. When her eyes met mine, she gave a small smile. "Got a minute?"

"Sure, Mama."

She shut the door then took a seat in the nook beside my vanity. She crossed her legs and sat with a straight spine, like she had to balance an invisible bowl upon her head. Her hands came together on her knee. "I just wanted to see if everything was alright."

"Why wouldn't it be?"

"Your father said you didn't want to train today."

"Oh...I was just tired."

"You've never been too tired before." Her stare was intrusive, like she could see behind my mask to the truth underneath. It was one of her supernatural mom abilities, when she could read my mind just with that powerful stare. "And your father said your eyes looked sad."

I guess my father was observant too.

Instead of interrogating me, she let the tense silence do all the work.

"Um...I was kinda seeing someone, but I'm not anymore." I didn't hide things from my mother, but I also didn't go out of my way to tell her details like this either. It wasn't ladylike of me to have lovers when I was a princess, so I did my best to keep that as secretive as possible. But my mother never scolded me for it. Once I'd reached a certain age, she'd stopped asking me these kinds of questions and respected my privacy.

"Are you okay?"

"I'll get over it."

"It's the artist, isn't it?"

Shit. "How—how did you know?"

"His sculpture."

I was going to kill that motherfucker. "Well—uh—yeah."

"Don't worry. Your father didn't notice. His mind is always somewhere else when he has those events."

"Thank the gods."

She gave a chuckle. "Sounds like an intense relationship."

"It was just physical." I avoided my mother's gaze as I said that.

"I hope I'm not making you uncomfortable, Harlow. You don't have to share any of this with me if you don't want to."

I turned back to her. "You aren't disappointed in me?"

"Why would I be?"

"Well…I mean…I'm not a virgin."

"You think I was a virgin when I met your father?" she asked with a slight laugh.

My eyebrows nearly popped off my face.

"I'd been with men before your father. I had a thing with one of my father's guards when I was your age. There's nothing you've done that I haven't done myself, Harlow. Don't be ashamed."

"Have I ever told you how cool you are?"

She smiled. "I'm cool now because you're an adult. But we butted heads *a lot* when you were little."

"Well, I was a brat."

"Not a brat," she said quickly. "Opinionated and hard-headed is how I would put it."

"Same thing."

She chuckled. "I was a pain in the ass too. So, why didn't it work out with Ethan?"

"I just didn't see it going anywhere."

"You're the one who ended it, then?"

"Yes."

"He must have been hurt."

"Yeah…I think he was. I feel bad."

"Don't," she said. "That's just how life is. He'll meet the right woman and forget all about you. And you'll find the right man at the right time."

"I didn't want it to end, but I didn't want to marry him either."

"That makes sense."

"It does?" I asked. "I feel like it makes no sense."

"It felt right at that moment in time, and you wanted that moment to last a lifetime. You should enjoy those moments while you can because when you meet your husband, they'll never come again. It's like having children. Enjoy that time before you're responsible for a family, not that you'll wish you didn't have a family when you do have them."

"It sounds like you're encouraging me to sleep around," I said with a laugh.

She gave a shrug. "How are you supposed to find your husband if you aren't putting yourself out there?"

"Father would lose his shit if he knew you were saying all this to me."

"No, he wouldn't. He suspected this was why you were upset today but didn't want to have the conversation himself. He's protective of you and your happiness, but he understands you're a grown woman entitled to these experiences at this time of your life."

"I never would have expected that."

"He'll never talk about it, but he understands."

I looked down at my hands, seeing the blisters I'd gotten that afternoon because I refused to wear gloves when we battled. "How did you know he was the one?"

Her eyes shifted away as her eyes glazed over with old memories. "It's not a moment or a thought. It's just a feeling that you get...and then you can't remember when you got that feeling because it seems like it's always been there."

"You guys are still in love."

"Oh, it gets better as you get older."

"It does?" I asked in surprise.

She gave a big nod. "Definitely."

"Even though you're old?"

She laughed. "Oh honey, we aren't old. Your father and I—"

"Okay, I know where this is going."

She chuckled. "It deepens and deepens. And just when you think it can't deepen any more, it does. And then when you have children, the connection is even more profound. You know, he wanted to have children long before I did. I had to make him wait."

"He's such a good father that I believe that."

"Yes, he's a good man," she said. "The best I know."

When I woke up the next morning, my muscles screamed with soreness. I may have held my own against my father, but I knew he wasn't lying in bed right now because he was too sore to move. "Ugh…" I finally got to my feet and walked to the windows, pulling the curtains open to reveal the golden morning. I went to the last window that had a view of the village, and the second I looked down, I noticed it.

A statue.

Made of white marble, it was smooth and finished, and it showed a pair of lovers locked in a passionate embrace. The man palmed her cheeks as he kissed her, her dress blowing in the invisible breeze, his arms bulging with strength from his craft. "Oh fuck."

I quickly got dressed then departed the castle without having breakfast. It was a morning routine I shared with my family, because my father got busier as the day went on, and most nights, he had dinner alone in his study. But I had to address this before he found out about it.

That would be *baaaaad*.

I nearly ran down the cobblestone streets to his shop. It was still early in the morning, so the streets were empty as people enjoyed their breakfasts in their homes. I turned the knob to let myself in, but it was locked. I tried the knob again, but it wouldn't budge. "Ethan!" I grabbed a pebble and chucked it at his window. The pebble bounced off so I grabbed another, and I must have thrown it too hard because the glass shattered. "Whoops…"

Ethan appeared a moment later, his hair tousled after a night of sleep. He was shirtless, and his tired eyes barely showed his annoyance. He gripped the windowsill and looked down at me, saying nothing because he knew exactly why I was there. Then he disappeared, probably to head downstairs and let me into the shop.

The door opened a moment later, and I stormed inside. "What the fuck, Ethan?" I rounded on him the second I was inside.

He gave a gentle push on the door then walked past me as he wiped the sleep from his eyes. He was in his lounge pants and nothing else, his strong back chiseled from all his hard work on his pieces.

"Hello?"

"I've been awake for two minutes."

"Oh, did I ruin your morning? Because my morning was ruined when I saw that damn statue beneath my window."

He dragged his hands down his face before he faced me head on. "Did you like it?"

"*Did I like it?*" I asked incredulously. "How did you even move it?"

"Answer the question."

"Ethan, you're the best artist Delacroix has ever had. Of course I love your work."

"Still didn't answer the question."

"No. It pissed me off—as you can see." I threw my arms around frantically.

"You're fully clothed—"

"That's not the point. You need to move it before someone sees it—like my father."

"I don't care if he sees it."

"Well, you really should."

"I don't care if he knows I love his daughter. I'll say it to his face."

I sighed as I dragged my hands down my face. "Ethan, stop this. You can't win me over with a sculpture—"

"You think another man would do that for you?"

"Not a man I want," I snapped.

His stony expression remained chiseled in his hard face.

"Stop this."

"I'm not a general or a soldier, but my art can inflict just as much pain as a blade. I'm worthy of you despite what you think."

"Ethan, it's not about worthiness—"

"We're great together, Harlow."

"Yes, we fuck really good, but that's it."

"I can have any woman I want, and you're telling me the only woman I actually do want doesn't want me?"

"A bit arrogant…"

"I can prove to your father that I'm worthy of his daughter."

"If I love you, you're already worthy—*but I don't*."

He stared at me like he hadn't heard any of that.

"I don't want to hurt you, but you're making me say these things. I just don't picture you as my husband. I'm sorry."

"You would if you gave it more time—"

"I don't need more time, Ethan. You just said you could have any woman you wanted. And you shouldn't waste your time on a woman who doesn't return your affections. After everything I've said to you, I don't deserve you. Be with a woman who does."

He continued to stare.

"Move the statue. *Now*." I stormed out of the shop and onto the street—and ran into a solid wall. My momentum shifted backward, and I almost fell right on my face in the street, but a strong arm gripped me and pulled me back.

"You alright?" A deep voice accompanied the strong grip.

My eyes lifted to the face in front of me, and I was so startled by his appearance I didn't speak. A second passed. I absorbed his stare, his fair skin, and his coffee-colored eyes. He had a sharp jawline covered in a shadow of hair, the same way my father wore his, always trimming it before it turned into a beard. Another second passed. I noticed his dark hair, short and slightly tousled. He was tall, much taller than me, tall like my father and brother. And his stare was so confident it was intimidating. "Yeah…I'm fine." I pulled my arm out of his grasp and stepped back like he was an enemy.

"You sure?" His eyes continued to study me, bright with intelligence.

"I said I'm fine," I snapped, angry for no reason at all.

"Heard a window break. Wanted to check on things."

"Oh…that was me."

"Why are you breaking windows?"

"It was an accident."

"How do you accidentally break a window?"

I stepped farther back, annoyed by the third degree. "Everything's fine. You can return to…wherever you came from." He wore dark clothes, all black, clothing that I didn't see others wear. It almost seemed regal, except there was no crest. I held his stare for another moment before I moved around him, keeping more space than necessary as if he might grab me again.

"You're angry, so it doesn't seem fine."

I could have just walked away and ignored him, but I halted. "I'm not angry."

"You should look in a mirror before you say that."

"Why do you care?" I snapped.

"Who said I did?"

My stare was locked on his face, seeing a man whose features made me pause. The high cheekbones, the powerful stare, the way his pupils were different from any other I'd seen. His presence felt both magnetic and terrifying.

I turned on my heel and walked away, determined to forget about the interaction that was now forever seared in my mind.

When I went to bed that night, the statue was gone.

Ethan must have retrieved it, and no one had witnessed the ridiculous display of affection. Dumping Ethan once was already hard enough, but dumping him a second time was even worse. I didn't want to hurt him—or myself.

A hurried knock sounded on my door the next morning. "Harlow?"

I recognized my mother's frantic voice. "It's open."

She opened the door and rushed into the room.

"What is it?" I kicked off the sheets and got to my feet, prepared to grab my sword even though we'd never been attacked.

"There are statues all around the castle—and right outside our bedroom."

"Oh shit."

"Harlow, he knows."

"Fuck."

"And Ethan has requested an audience with your father."

I gripped my head as I stood back. "This is not happening."

"I thought you ended things with him."

"I did—*twice*."

"Well, Ethan didn't get the message."

"He won't let me break up with him. *Literally*."

"You need to hurry," she said. "Because your father is about to meet him in his study."

"This is not happening." I rushed across my bedroom and grabbed whatever I could find. "Not happening." I pulled on my boots and nearly tipped over. "I tell him it's over, and he decides to speak to my father? Who does that?"

"A man about to propose."

I stilled as I looked at her. "No."

My mother gave a slight shrug. "What else would it be?"

I burst through the door to my father's study and found Ethan sitting in the armchair that faced my father's desk.

My father sat there—and he'd never looked more uncomfortable. His eyes shifted to me, his hard face stoic like he was stuck at a dinner party he wanted to escape.

When Ethan saw me, he rose to his feet.

There was so much I wanted to say but couldn't in front of my father, so I whispered, "What are you doing?"

Ethan's eyes turned back to my father. "My bloodline isn't tied to royalty. I have no connections to the aristocracy. My father tilled the earth until the blisters on his hands popped. My mother has sewn clothes and pricked her fingers until they bled. Just like them, my hands are my craft. I've produced the best pieces for the halls in your castle, made powerful statues to warn our enemies when they march on our gates. I don't have a lot to offer your daughter, but my hands will provide a life for her. My heart is in my hands, and every sculpture I produce is in her likeness, because there is no woman more beautiful than she."

This was mortifying.

"King Rolfe, I ask for your daughter's hand in marriage—"

"*Ethan.*"

He ignored me and looked at my father.

My father stared at him for a long time before his eyes shifted to me.

I wanted to die.

He rose to his feet behind his desk, his shoulders enormous and his cloak long. "My daughter doesn't need my permission to marry a man she loves. I raised my daughter as I raised my son—to make her own decisions without outside opinion or approval. So, she's the one you should be asking—not me."

Ethan turned to me, his eyes victorious.

I could feel the storm clouds gather in my eyes. "I told you your station had nothing to do with this."

"Ask my daughter to marry you."

My eyes remained on Ethan, but goose bumps formed on my skin when I heard my father's tone.

"*Ask her.*"

Ethan swallowed, probably because he'd picked up on the hostility too. "Harlow—"

"No."

The silence was so heavy it was difficult to breathe.

"You shouldn't have come here," I whispered.

My father came around his desk. "My daughter has given her answer. Our business has concluded." He approached Ethan and looked at him head on, his eyes sharp as arrows. "Harass my daughter again, and it'll be the last thing you ever do." My father didn't raise his voice, but the walls shook anyway. It was a silent blow, a knife slipped between the ribs. "*Leave.*"

Ethan departed the study immediately.

I should have felt better now that he was gone, but standing with my father was somehow infinitely worse. Tense. Awkward. Unbearable. My father didn't look at me at all, like this was all a horrible nightmare he wanted to forget. "I'm sorry—"

"You owe no apology." His eyes finally shifted back to mine.

"He's not a bad guy—"

"He's a man who doesn't know how to handle a broken heart," he said. "He's willing to do anything and everything to get back what he lost, but he needs to face the truth—that you were never his to lose."

I'd never heard my father speak that way.

"Your mother and I agreed that she would handle this part of your life. It's not my place, and I don't want it to be my place. But having a daughter who's not only beautiful but smart and fierce will have consequences—and I'm not ignorant to that."

I didn't know what to say.

"Tell me if he bothers you again. I'll handle it."

"I don't need you to handle it, Father."

His eyes shifted away, and he released a quiet sigh. "Your uncle is on his way for a visit."

"He is?" I asked in excitement, grateful for the change in subject. "What about Grandmother? And Lila?"

"Only Uncle Ian."

"Well, that's still exciting."

"He should be here in the morning." My father looked at his desk. "I have matters that require my attention. Is there anything else?" It was still awkward. Really awkward.

"No."

He turned to his desk and got back to work, wanting to move past the tension as quickly as possible.

I walked out and shut the door behind me, wanting to forget the horror of this day.

3

AURELIAS

On the roof of the building, I sat and looked up into her window. She was too far away for her emotions to transfer into my mind, but I could read the emotions in her body as she moved back and forth, pacing with her arms crossed over her chest, her eyes on the ground near her feet.

I had watched Ethan position the sculptures the night before, place them in front of the castle as the guards watched on in confusion. He erected them all around the castle, and after seeing her, I knew they were made in her likeness.

And I knew she didn't like it.

When she'd entered his shop, I could feel the swelling of her rage, feel the fury from her tiny little body. When I'd arrived in Delacroix, I'd thought this mission would be straightforward. Just grab Princess Harlow and leave. But she made it complicated.

I watched her train with her father—taking on a man twice her size with far more experience. Instead of being a spoiled member of royalty, she dedicated her time to Delacroix, gathering feedback from the villagers so King Rolfe could make improvements in the city to make their lives better. King Rolfe had relocated the capital to Delacroix during his reign in deference to his wife, who had grown up in and loved the city. Unlike other magistrates, this royal family served their people—rather than the other way around.

I almost felt bad for what I was about to do.

Almost.

I watched her approach the window then look down to where the statue had been days ago. She didn't notice me, her mind distracted by all her distress. When she'd bumped into me outside the shop, it was a test.

A test of her reaction.

She was angry from her conversation with her lover, or her *former* lover, so there was a swirl of emotions inside her. She was angry, frustrated to the point of tears, but when her eyes locked on mine there was a momentary pause.

A break in the clouds.

A ray of sunshine.

A glimmer of attraction.

I couldn't drag her by force, not when she was so skilled with the blade and could easily cause a scene. I'd have to get her alone, slip something into her food or drink, and then get her out of Delacroix without being seen.

I couldn't believe I'd agreed to his bullshit…kidnapping a princess. It was insulting. My brother better have healed all of the kingdoms by now and wiped the Ethereal off the face of the fucking earth. He was playing the hero, and I was stuck cleaning the stables. Was nearly killed by a yeti for this shit.

My mind started to drift as I became lost in my bitterness, but all those thoughts were wiped clean when I noticed the bare skin that appeared. My eyes focused on the window, seeing her pull her dress over her head. It happened fast, her tight tummy on display along with her perky tits. But then she stepped out of view, and when she returned, she'd changed into something else.

All my complaints and annoyance disappeared at the sight of her rosy flesh. She was a pretty girl, no denying that, but I was used to a line of beautiful women who were desperate to please me. But it still made me pause, still made my world stop for a moment in time.

Perhaps being alone with her wouldn't be so unbearable.

4

HUNTLEY

My scouts sighted Pyre far in the distance, so I left the castle and stepped into the clearing where he would land with my brother. Ivory came with me, wearing a uniform similar to mine because she only wore dresses for social events—and wore nothing when it was just the two of us.

Pyre's scales were brilliant in the sunlight, and the creature was more magnificent than I remembered. Powerful wings lowered him through the air, and when his sharp talons hit the ground, the earth shook. Ian sat at the nape of his neck and gripped the reins for balance before he toppled forward.

Ian climbed off Pyre and hit the dirt, wearing his black uniform with his armor, a jacket made of fur with a cloak across his back. It was far colder in HeartHolme than it was in Delacroix. His eyes locked with mine, and he approached, his arms swinging, his cloak moving in the breeze behind him.

I couldn't suppress the grin that crept on to my lips.

He couldn't either.

When he reached me, he skipped the handshake and the diplomacy and gave me a bear hug.

I was ready for it, so I gripped him tightly and gave him a hard pat on the back. "I'll provide a step stool for you next time."

Ian laughed as he shoved me off him. "Good. I'll shove it up your ass." He turned to Ivory next, and the hug he gave her was far gentler, and it was accompanied by a quick kiss on the temple. "Long time, no see."

"How's your family?"

"Good."

"Good."

Ian turned back to me. "Let's speak in private."

"That's not a good sign."

He gave a nod toward the castle so we could depart.

Ivory moved to Pyre, stroking his nose as they brought their heads close together. Decades had passed, but their connection had remained as strong as ever.

Ian and I returned to the castle and walked down the hallway to my study.

"How's Mother?" I asked.

"Immortal."

I chuckled. "Not slowing down?"

"I'm starting to think she'll never slow down. Her mind is still sharp as a tack."

"You'll probably die before her and never be King of HeartHolme."

He smirked. "I wouldn't be surprised."

We entered my study and shut the door. Ian helped himself to the decanter on my desk and poured himself a glass. He dropped his heavy coat and tossed it over an empty chair before he tugged off his gloves. "How are things in Delacroix and the Kingdoms?"

"Lots of parties and bullshit."

He dropped into the chair with his glass, that smirk still there. "You need to learn how to have fun."

"Talking to ass-kissers isn't my idea of fun." I took a drink.

He shook his head. "Good thing you have Ivory."

She did all the talking, and I just stood there. My only concern was the safety of my people. Everything else seemed unimportant.

"How are the little ones?"

"Little ones?" I asked. "Atticus is a man, and Harlow... She's not little anymore." It pained me to say it, to step into this new stage of my children's lives. They had been such a handful when they were little, keeping me up all night and dependent on me for every little thing, but now, I'd give anything to go back to those early days.

"Long nights, short years." He took a drink. "Mother was right."

"Harlow had an...incident." I hadn't even discussed this with Ivory because it was hard to speak about it.

"What kind of incident?"

"You remember Ethan?"

"The artist, right?"

"Very talented young man. But he's become a bit obsessed with my daughter."

Ian turned serious, understanding the discomfort since he had a daughter of his own.

"He asked for her hand."

His eyebrows shot straight up. "Shit. What did you say—"

"I let her answer herself."

"What'd she say?"

"No."

"Fuck...that's awkward."

"I think she and Ethan had...*a relationship*...and when she tried to leave, he decided to fight harder."

Ian masked his discomfort with another drink. "What was his plan? To get your approval to convince her to stay?"

"I don't know. The less I know, the better."

"I'm surprised you didn't kill him."

"I wanted to." I sat behind the desk, my curled knuckles underneath my jaw. The fireplace was cold because it'd been too warm for a fire. But most nights, Ivory would come for a visit while I worked, and I'd take her on the desk while the flames warmed my back. "But Ivory had a talk with me a couple years ago."

"What kind of talk?"

"The birds and the bees—the father edition."

Ian didn't make any jokes, probably because he understood perfectly.

"I've looked the other way and stayed out of her business. Never asked her a single question about her personal life. Worked pretty well—until Ethan marched in here and got me involved."

"That sucks."

"That's why I want to kill him. He forced my head out of the sand."

He took another drink.

"What about Lila?"

"My head is buried deeper in the sand than yours."

"I remember how we used to be when we were that age. Makes me sick."

"Yeah."

"But she's my wife's daughter, and I know she's smart—too smart for her own good. Too smart to get her heart broken. Too smart to settle for a lesser man. I have faith that the man she chooses will be one whom I like."

He swirled his glass and said nothing.

We remained that way for a while, just sitting in silence.

"What news do you bring?" I finally asked. "How's HeartHolme?"

"Cold," he said. "It's always fucking cold."

"The Teeth?"

"They stay on their lands and never violate the pact."

"Good."

"But there was a ship a while ago."

My eyes narrowed on his face.

"It was sailing away by the time scouts notified me. The wood was dark, almost black, but with flecks of gold that reflected the light, a kind of ship none have ever seen before. Its sails were black too, like it was meant to sail only in darkness. We launched a fleet to search for it, but we never found it again."

I digested every word. "The outcasts?"

"Maybe."

"They were sailing away from us?"

"Yes."

"Which means they got whatever they wanted and left."

"I suppose."

"Did you take Pyre and search?"

"I did, and he saw nothing."

"Your scouts didn't report someone moving at the bottom of the cliffs?"

He shook his head. "There was one time when two yetis were roaring in the middle of the night, not from the mountains, but the valley. A search party was sent in the morning, and they eventually came across their bodies, bloody and defeated by blades."

"It's not easy to take down a yeti, let alone two."

"I agree."

"Even a ship full of people would have had a hard time."

"I agree."

I continued to stare at my brother, my mind working furiously to unlock the mystery. "Where were the bodies discovered?"

"About fifty leagues east of our camp."

"So, closer to the Teeth."

"I would say halfway."

My blood ran cold. "You think they're planning something?"

"I doubt they would invite someone to their lands and risk getting caught."

"Unless they didn't invite anyone…and they came of their own accord."

Ian was about to take a drink, but he lowered his glass instead. "Who?"

"I don't know…"

"There's only one way to find out. We speak to Rancor. If we're right, he knows we're onto him and might abandon whatever he's plotting. If we aren't right, then he knows we're still suspicious of him and haven't dropped our guard."

After I considered it for a long time in silence, I gave a nod. "These past decades of peace have been the best of my life. I'm not going to let the Teeth squander it."

5

HARLOW

I sat at the bar with Brianna, the two of us enjoying a beer along with a bowl of nuts. Patrons at the tables enjoyed the stew from the kitchens, turning their evening festivities into dinner. Others sat alone at the bar and drank after a hard day of work. Fires burned in the hearth, the only light in the dark place.

"So, it's really over?" Brianna asked. She was a seamstress who had worked on my clothes for the last few years. We'd struck up a friendship and had become good friends over the years.

"Yes."

"Ethan is so hot, though."

"I know," I said with a sigh. "But he fucked it up when he made it complicated."

"I can't believe he asked your father to marry you."

"Idiot."

"Another king would have beheaded him just for the insult. Ethan's lucky your father is composed and doesn't have a temper."

"Oh...he has a temper." He just didn't show it in front of Atticus and me.

"Have you spoken to Ethan since?"

"My father threatened to kill him if he bothered me. Looks like Ethan took that threat seriously. It was supposed to just be for fun, but he screwed it all up."

"He's an artist. He's emotional and gets attached to things."

I grabbed my beer and took a drink.

"What a shame... He was so hot."

"Are you asking my permission, Brianna?"

"No," she said with a laugh, but she immediately reached for the nuts and avoided my gaze. "I wouldn't do that to you."

"Girl, go for it."

"What?" she asked incredulously.

"I'm the one who ended things, so I have no claim to the guy."

After she ate a few nuts, she looked at me again. "You're serious."

"Yes. He's great in bed—so I recommend him."

She suddenly became distracted because her eyes moved across the room, like she was watching someone walk behind me. Then her gaze turned steady over my shoulder. "I bet *he's* good in bed…"

"Who?"

"A hot motherfucker just sat at the bar."

"A hot motherfucker?" I asked. "Never heard that one before."

"He's super-hot, alright?" Brianna said. "I don't know how else to say it."

I started to turn.

She grabbed my wrist. "Don't make it obvious. He's looking this way."

I pushed her hand off. "Psh, I don't care if he knows I'm looking." I swiveled in the stool and followed Brianna's gaze. "I want to take a look at this hot motherfucker." My eyes found him right away, broad shoulders stretching the fabric of his shirt, pronounced cords up his neck, eyes as dark as coal. It only took me a second to recognize him, seeing his eyes meet mine across the room.

I turned back to Brianna and covered my unease with a drink of my beer.

"Told you."

"I've met him before."

"You know him?" she asked in surprise.

"Well, *met* might not be the right word. I bumped into him once. He was kinda an asshole. A hot asshole."

"Those are the best kind."

"They are…"

"Are you going to talk to him?"

"Is he still sitting alone?"

"Yes—and he's staring at you."

"Are you sure he's not staring at you?" I asked.

"Yep," she said. "Hundred percent. Gonna go for it?"

"What if you pay Ethan a visit, and I dig my claws into this guy?"

"Oooh, that sounds like a plan. Then we'll have breakfast and spill the tea."

"Perfect."

She finished off the rest of her beer then left the stool. "Hope you get some."

"You too." I watched her walk out before I swiveled in the stool to face forward. Instead of walking over to him right away, I decided to sit there and take my time, give him a chance to come to me first. I didn't mind making the first move, but I preferred to be chased.

"Is this seat taken?"

Nooooooo.

A man appeared at my side, his beer already on the bar because he intended to occupy the stool whether I agreed or not. He wasn't bad to look at, but compared to the hot motherfucker, he was plain. "Uh..."

He took a seat. "Jacob. What's your name?"

Some people knew who I was on sight, but not all. My father was recognizable to all, however. "I don't want to hurt your feelings, but—"

"Hey, baby." Hot motherfucker appeared, his eyes on me for a moment before they shifted to the man who was trying to pick me up. He didn't say another word, but his hostility was as loud as a scream.

"My apologies." Jacob grabbed his beer and returned to wherever he'd come from.

He dropped onto the stool that was reserved for him, tapped his fingers on the counter to get the barmaiden's attention, and ordered another beer. She abandoned everything she was doing and gave it to him right away, like she'd noticed him the way Brianna had.

He took a drink before he pivoted in the stool slightly so our eyes met.

I stared, my fingers around my glass. My heart raced. My hands suddenly felt clammy. I hadn't had butterflies in my stomach since I was sixteen, but now they were back in full force.

His dark eyes stared at me with calmness, like this meeting didn't provoke him nearly as much as it did me. Confident and suave, he wasn't fazed by a pretty girl the way his sexiness fazed me.

I forced a poker face and feigned my usual confidence. "How did you know I wasn't interested? Maybe I was."

"Would you rather talk to a boy or a man?"

Yep...he was a hot asshole. "Who's the boy and who's the man?"

He didn't let my comment catch him off-balance. A small, knowing smirk moved over his lips before he grabbed his beer and took a drink. "This tastes like piss."

"Then why are you drinking it?"

"They're out of scotch."

My father drank the same thing. There were always bottles in his study. I tried not to stare too hard, to force my eyes on my drink or across the bar, to act natural. But when I was this nervous, it was hard to even remember what normalcy looked like.

"Break any more windows lately?" He leaned slightly against the bar, his arm resting there, his bicep and forearm exposed beneath the sleeve. His arms were like his neck, covered in rivers that disappeared into the mountains of his muscles. His skin was fair like he didn't have a laborious job outside, but rather something indoors that protected him from the sunshine.

I was so distracted by his appearance that I forgot the question he'd asked. "Sorry?"

That arrogant smirk returned. "I heard you break hearts the way you break windows."

Word had spread like wildfire. Everyone had seen the statues Ethan erected around the castle and connected the dots. When people asked him about it, he must have told the truth—that I'd rejected his marriage proposal. "I don't know what you heard, but I'm not a bitch. I mean, I am, but not that *kind* of bitch."

That partial smile remained on his lips, and his eyes flashed with a hint of intrigue. "I heard the artist was deeply in love with you and asked the king for your hand, but you said no."

"That's all true, but there's more to the story."

He never questioned me, only silently prodded for more information.

"Have you ever been in a relationship that you knew had no future, but you wanted to stay anyway? At least for a little while."

He considered the question for a long stretch of silence. A stretch so long, it seemed like nothing would follow. "No."

"Well, that's how it was. I knew he wouldn't be my husband, but that didn't mean I wanted it to end so soon. But he wanted something more serious, and I just wanted to fuck."

His smile dropped, and now his stare hardened.

"I'm sure you've been in plenty of those relationships... or *situationships*."

He neither confirmed nor denied it.

"Wow, a gentleman."

"Oh, trust me. I'm not."

Damn, I loved a "*I don't give a fuck*" attitude on guys. My weakness. An asshole who said he was an asshole straight to your face. A guy so confident that he could get you without even trying.

"Ethan fucked up a good thing."

"Yeah, he did."

"But it worked out for me." With that confident stare, he lifted his glass to his lips and took a drink, stare on me all the while. Only a few guys could pull off confidence like that, and he was one of them.

"Why haven't I seen you around before?" I spent a lot of my time in the village. I didn't know everyone, but if I'd ever seen him on the street before, I would have remembered. There was no way I would have seen this drop-dead gorgeous man and forgotten about him. If I didn't go home with him tonight, I knew his memory would stay with me.

"I moved to Delacroix a month ago."

"What do you do?"

"Private loans. When the farmers have a poor harvest, I loan them money and charge them interest. I fund other projects, like homes and buildings. I've done it in the other kingdoms and thought I'd make my mark here."

That meant he had money, but he wasn't a member of royalty or the aristocracy. Perhaps his family had handed down their wealth through the generations. "Impressive."

"Not as impressive as you."

I felt a flutter in my chest. "What's so impressive about me?"

"Your skill with the blade." When my eyebrows furrowed, he continued. "I saw you train with your father on the field. You're good. Better than most men."

"How would you know?" I asked before I took a drink. "If you're just a banker…"

That smile returned. "You can't take a compliment."

"Yes, I can. I just wasn't expecting *that* compliment."

"Then what were you expecting? That I tell you how painstakingly beautiful you are? That your ass makes me hard every time I see it? That you have tits that my dick wants to fuck?" He said all those perverse things with the same tone he would use to describe the weather, pulled it off when any other guy would get slapped across the face. "I thought that compliment would be better received."

I felt the heat burn the skin of my cheeks. Without seeing my reflection, I knew they were rose-red, like a sunburn after a long day outside. My stomach was tight as my core strengthened in preparation for something...whatever it was.

"Or perhaps you prefer the latter." He took another drink then licked his lips.

"You're an asshole."

That grin was back.

"But luckily for you...I like assholes."

We entered his home, a modest two-story cottage with a stone fireplace. There was a fire in the hearth when we walked in the door, shadows in the corners of the soft glow. I should have taken a look around and issued a compliment, but I really didn't give a fuck about his house right now.

When I turned around, his shirt was already off and tossed aside. Built like a mountain but shredded, he was six-foot-something of masculine beauty, with powerful shoulders, sexy arms, and eyes more intense than a hurricane. Ethan was hot…but not *this* hot. "Oh fuck…" My eyes admired his chest then slowly moved down, counting all the muscles there, all eight of them.

He came at me and lifted me by the ass, putting me on the kitchen counter so he could stand between my knees. He tugged me toward him so his lips could catch mine. His kiss was hard like the rest of him, demanding and violent.

Exactly how I liked it.

My arms circled his neck, and my fingers felt his short strands. My tits were against his chest, but my clothing concealed my skin from him. I hadn't inherited my father's height, so this man was much taller than me, by over a foot, maybe almost two, so sitting on the counter gave me the opportunity to kiss him without craning my neck.

He took my mouth with desperation, biting my bottom lip before turning his head slightly to land another purposeful kiss on my lips. He set the pace, his hand sliding deep into my hair as he positioned my face the way he wanted. He knew what he wanted and took it from me, his fingers fisting my hair possessively.

My thighs squeezed his hips as my fingers explored his shoulders, feeling the separation of muscle with the lines of strength. I touched his arms too, moaning into his mouth when I felt the cords on top of the muscles.

He gripped my shirt and yanked it over my head, exposing my lacy white bra underneath. Without breaking our kiss, he reached my spine and snapped it open like he'd done it a hundred times. The lace bra dropped into my lap, and his big hands gripped both of my tits with such force it actually hurt. He didn't treat me like a delicate piece of china that could break. He treated me like the steel of a sword, a weapon too strong to bend or shatter.

I liked that.

My fingers reached for his pants and got them open, yanking everything over his hips so his cock would come free.

I broke our kiss to look.

His lips immediately moved for my neck, kissing me as he trailed them toward my ear.

He exceeded my expectations—by a long shot.

"You like what you see, baby?"

My arm hooked around his neck as my lips found his again. "Fuck yes."

"Wait until you feel it." He scooped me off the counter and carried me to the couch in front of the fire. His pants were around his thighs, but that didn't impede his stride. He dropped me in the corner and kicked off his boots and pants until he was naked, his long legs chiseled and strong, covered in swirls of dark hair. His dick was groomed, like he expected people to look at it often.

I'd had a lot of good sex in my life, but I knew this would be the best.

He tugged my trousers and panties down to my ankles before he yanked off my boots. He tugged again, getting everything off until it was just my bare skin. He grabbed my ankles and dragged me down before his knees dropped onto the couch cushions. He moved over me, snug between my thighs, his powerful body on top of mine. His chest covered me like a rain cloud, and then his hands gripped my ass cheeks and adjusted my hips so he could slide inside.

My hands planted on his chest as his lips swooped down to catch mine. His tongue came into my mouth and touched mine, tangling them together in the most erotic dance. This man hadn't even fucked me yet, but he was the best lay of my life. He was the best kisser too, so the number of girls in his bed must have far exceeded the number of men in mine.

One of my legs was pinned to the back of the couch with his shoulder, while my other leg hung off the edge. He deepened the angle of my hips and opened me to him before he slid his fingers inside me.

I breathed into his mouth when I felt him, expecting his dick instead of his big fingers.

He pulsed inside me as he kissed me, giving a sexy moan when he felt how wet I was.

I wasn't even embarrassed.

He twisted his fingers as his thumb found my nub. He rubbed that too, his touch hot like a strike of lightning. In a circular motion, he rubbed harder and harder, getting my hips to grind. My hand cupped his face, and I moaned into his mouth, slowly inching toward the explosion that had started to build.

He removed his fingers, and the absence of his touch was like ice. But I heard the sound of his wet fingers against his length and saw the way he covered himself in my arousal, lubricating the head so he could shove that big dick inside me.

Our lips were close together, but now it was all hot breaths and wet body parts. He fingered me again and rubbed more on himself, coating his dick to the base.

My nails started to claw his skin because I was so anxious. My own arousal turned me on even more, knowing I was wetter for him than I'd ever been for anyone else. "Fuck me, asshole."

A partial smile moved on to his lips before he grabbed his base and directed his dick at my entrance. His head was too big to fit easily, so he had to push several times to break past my tight lips. But with another thrust, he made it, and then he sank nice and slow, moaning at my tightness. His previous guard was dropped as he succumbed to the pleasure between my legs. Another moan escaped as a gruff sound, and he pounded me into the corner of the couch, my little body sinking farther between the cushions and the armrest.

My hands touched his back, felt all the distinct muscles underneath the skin as I pulled him into me, getting fucked like an animal. It was hard and fast right from the beginning, and he didn't have to stop and go, to edge himself because he couldn't keep his load contained. His body was a blanket over mine, his stare dark and intense.

Fuck, it was good.

I was relaxed, knowing I would come without trying, that he could control himself until I was finished so I could take my time and enjoy it. He had such a big dick, and it felt even bigger when he slammed into me like that, his balls hitting my ass over and over. Our heavy breaths grew louder, and the moans blurred into those breaths.

"Come on, baby." He worked up a sweat when he fucked me this hard and this long. He just kept going, his dick trained better than a dog.

"Go a little longer, and I'll let you come inside me."

"Fuck…" He released another gruff sound then stopped, his eyes closing in concentration.

My hand grabbed his ass, and I tugged him into me, wanting him to keep going. "You want to come inside me?"

He kept his eyes closed, his dick so hard within my body.

"Then earn it." My hand cupped his cheek, and I forced his stare on me.

His eyes opened, and his stare could kill.

"And maybe if you do a really good job, I'll let you come in my ass—"

"*For fuck's sake.*" He slammed into me again, fucking me harder than he did before, doing his damnedest to make me come as quickly as possible.

I'd been on the verge from the second he'd rubbed my clit, but I edged myself on purpose, wanting to make it last and torture him at the same time. I'd had good sex, but most of the time, we took a lot of breaks because the guy couldn't hold his load. This one could, and I wanted to push him to his breaking point.

"Harder." My nails dug into his ass.

He was already giving me his all, every one of his sexy muscles working hard to move deep inside me.

"You're doing this on purpose," he said against my lips.

"Yes."

He released a moan, like he was turned on more than pissed off.

That sound was too much to ignore, and I couldn't fight the urge anymore. The explosion was instantaneous, hitting me hard without warning, making me scream from the corner of the couch where I was buried. "Fuck…yes." It was sensational, scorching, the best climax I'd ever had.

He kept his pace as I writhed in pleasure, doing his job to make it last as long as possible. But once my cries subsided and my breaths turned heavy, he slowed down slightly, right at the finish line.

My eyes locked on his. "Come inside me…"

The moan he released nearly sounded angry. With his final pumps, he filled me, the cords in his neck tightening, his face flushing red. He had been sexy from across the bar, but he was even sexier when he fucked.

I tugged on his ass and kept him inside me. "You earned it."

He finished, his breathing short and irregular, his hips bucking uncontrollably. "Yes…" He filled me with all of him, forcing himself inside to give me every drop. His breaths remained strained even when he was finished, and his dick didn't soften at all.

It felt so good to be so full.

Then he did what I least expected and started to fuck me again.

I'd never seen a guy do that, stay rock hard for another round and take me as aggressively the second time, as if the first round had been a fucking appetizer before the main course. "Fuck yes…"

I lay there awhile and dozed off.

The couch was small and he was a big guy, so we were forced to be close together, cuddling like we were bonded by love rather than lust. When I opened my eyes, my thigh was hooked over his hips, and my face was against his hard chest. I blinked a few times before I turned to look at the room. It was still dark, moonlight coming through the open curtains. I didn't know how much time had passed, fifteen minutes or several hours, but I knew I had to get home. I tried to slide free and not wake him, but I was the one pinned against the back of the couch. I managed to sit up and crawl to the other side, but then he woke up.

He looked at me before he released a quiet sigh and propped his arm behind his head. His eyes were drooped and heavy, and the sleepiness looked sexy on him somehow. He was still naked, and his dick lay there, impressive even when it wasn't hard. "Trying to sneak out?" He spoke with a deep voice, deeper than usual because he was still half asleep.

"Trying and failing." I grabbed my panties from the rug and pulled them on.

He sat up and rubbed one eye with his palm, his hair messy from the way I'd fingered it in the throes of passion. "Let me get you some water."

"I'm good." I found my pants next and pulled them up.

He pulled on his bottoms and headed to the kitchen to get a glass of water.

I followed him, not because I wanted that drink, but because I needed my bra and shirt.

He set the water on the counter.

I ignored it.

He stood behind the counter and stared, his hands gripping the edge.

I clasped my bra then pulled my shirt on before I fixed my hair. I had to sneak back into the castle, and if I got caught, I didn't want to look like I'd been fucked like a whore in a brothel. There would be no punishment for the crime, but it was still awkward. "Goodnight." I headed to the front door.

His footsteps sounded behind me. "I can escort you."

"I can escort myself." I grabbed the handle and pulled the door open, but it only opened a crack before it stopped. My eyes lifted to his hand above my head, the obstacle that blocked my exit. "It's late and I'm tired." I shut the door then turned to look at him. "And we don't have to do the *thing*."

"We do have to do the *thing* because I want to see you again."

My eyes narrowed. "What happened to being an asshole?"

A slow smirk moved on to his lips. "That hasn't changed, baby. We made a deal."

"What deal?"

He moved closer to me, the lines of his muscles pronounced even in the dark. "If I fucked you good, I have the honor of fucking you in the ass."

"That was just dirty talk—"

"How many times did I make you come?" He came closer, pushing my back into the door, his face looming over mine.

My breathing picked up as my eyes remained locked on his.

"Answer me."

"You are an asshole."

That smirk deepened. "A deal's a deal, baby. Or are you not a woman of your word?"

"Don't manipulate me—"

"I expect you here tomorrow night. And if you don't show up, I'll come find you."

"Good luck with that." I shoved him in the chest so I could get the door open then stormed out.

6

HARLOW

I joined my family for breakfast the next morning, doing my best to pretend I wasn't utterly exhausted from the night before. Makeup covered the bags under my eyes, but it couldn't mask the fatigue I felt all over my body. He did all the fucking and I just lay there, but I felt like I'd run across all the Kingdoms in a single day.

My father sat at the head of the table as always, and Uncle Ian was on his right. Their plates were full of farm-fresh scrambled eggs, strips of bacon and sausage, whole-wheat toast, and roasted potatoes.

My mother sat on my father's other side, having a meager plate of assorted fruit.

"So, there were three kings?" Atticus asked, wanting to hear about the defeat of Necrosis for the hundredth time.

"Yes," Uncle Ian said. "And they were all bastards."

"We would have lost that war without the dragons," Father said. "When your mother and I arrived in HeartHolme, that battle was lost…until they unleashed their fire."

"I don't understand what Necrosis is," Atticus said. "They're undead creatures?"

"It doesn't matter what they were," Uncle Ian said as he took a bite of bacon. "They're long gone now."

One of the servants brought me a plate, a bowl of oatmeal sprinkled with brown sugar. Unlike my father and brother, I couldn't just eat whatever I wanted and keep my petite size. The men scarfed down their food like their stomachs were bottomless pits.

"You look tired." Mom pressed her hand to the middle of my back, her question affectionate rather than accusatory.

"Yeah…didn't sleep well." Or at all…

"Well, after training with your father this afternoon, you should sleep well tonight." Her fingers moved through my strands of hair before she returned her hand to the table to finish her breakfast.

"We should spar," Atticus said, looking at me from across the table. "I'm curious to see if you're as good as everyone says."

"No." That was all my father said, his arms on the table, eating without manners.

Atticus glanced at my father at the head of the table. "Why? You spar with her—"

"If you ever strike your sister, I'll strike you." He paused to stare at my brother, to give him that look that said it would be stupid to cross him.

Atticus looked at me then gave a subtle shrug.

"Uncle Ian, I was disappointed you didn't bring Lila with you," I said, stirring my spoon in the bowl.

"She's occupied with her studies right now," Uncle Ian said before he drank his coffee. "Maybe next time."

We ate in silence for the next few minutes, not the awkward and uncomfortable kind most people experienced. We were so acquainted with one another that the silence was as comforting as a riveting conversation.

Then my father spoke. "I'll be joining Uncle Ian when he returns to HeartHolme. It's been a while since I've seen my mother."

"Is something wrong?" I blurted. "Is she okay?"

"Never better," Uncle Ian said. "In better shape than me, honestly."

"But she can't make the trip to Delacroix any longer, and it's been a while since I've visited her," Father said. "I have obligations as a king—and I also have obligations as a son. I hope you remember that when I'm gone and you're all your mother has."

Atticus rolled his eyes. "You talk about your death every day, I swear."

"You do," I said in agreement. "It's annoying."

He focused on his food. "Death comes swiftly in the dark. It's like a shadow. You don't see it until it's standing right behind you. All I ask is you learn from my example and take care of your mother as you've watched me take care of mine."

Mother stopped eating her fruit and stared at Father, her elbows on the table and her hands together. She was quiet, but her piercing look carried a conversation entirely on its own.

When Father ignored her stare, I knew there was trouble in paradise.

"When do you leave?" I asked.

"Tomorrow," Father answered. "Your mother will rule in my stead while I'm gone."

"Good," Atticus said. "That means things will lighten up around here."

I swallowed my chuckle.

Uncle Ian let a smirk slip through.

Father ignored the insults and continued to eat, but his face was as hard as his stare.

7

IVORY

The door to his study was slightly ajar, so I stuck my head inside to look at my husband, The King of Delacroix and the Kingdoms.

He sat at his desk, his elbow on the armrest with his curled fingers against his chin. He stared at the cold fireplace with eyes that didn't blink, his thoughts heavy like an anchor at the bottom of the sea. He sat there for over a minute, and it took even longer for him to blink. His attention was focused like a hawk on its prey—so I knew his mind was full of insecurities.

I entered his study, and that was when his eyes flicked to mine.

"What is it, baby?" He dropped his hand from his chin and straightened, like he'd been caught doing something he shouldn't.

I approached his desk, seeing the same man I'd fallen in love with decades ago. Time had changed his features slightly, but he still had eyes so blue they rivaled the sky in spring. His eyes and mouth were still hard, and his jawline had the sharpness of a blade because he remained fit even though peace had reigned since before our babies were born. Most kings grew fat and lazy as they kept their thrones warm, but Huntley was prepared for battle like a siege was just a league away. His arms were still thick and strong, and his shoulders stretched out everything he wore. He had the body of a young man in his prime, but he had the sexiness of a man who had aged like a fine wine.

I did my best to keep up with his commitment, but after giving him two children, my body was soft in places where it used to be hard. But he kissed my scars like they turned him on and spanked my ass like he'd bought me for the night. Kings had mistresses—but my husband only had me.

He continued his stare, waiting for my response.

"You lied to me."

His expression didn't change, hard and defiant as always.

"And I thought we didn't do that to each other."

He was so still that he had turned to stone. Breaths didn't even raise his chest because he stopped breathing at the accusation.

"You only stare at the fireplace like that if something troubles you."

His eyes finally dropped, and he released an annoyed sigh.

"The last time you did it was when Harlow was born prematurely, and all you could do was sit in that chair and think."

He continued to avoid my stare, plotting his next move now that he'd been caught.

"What's the real reason you're traveling to HeartHolme?"

He stared at the fireplace a moment longer before he rose out of his chair and came around the desk, speaking to me like an equal, not a ruler to an inferior. He always treated me this way, as someone who shared the crown rather than as a woman who'd only given him children. "That's between Ian and me."

My arms slid over my chest and my head cocked when he defied me. "Excuse me?"

"You heard me." A foot taller than me and regal in his uniform, he was intimidating, even if he was my husband.

"And you expect me to accept that—"

"I can't say, baby."

"And I can't accept that, Huntley."

He stared me down.

I met that stare with my own hostility. "You asked me to rule in your stead. That means I should be privy to your plans. To deceive me means you're either arrogant or—"

"I don't want you to worry." His voice dropped, turning soft the way it did when he made love to me or spoke to Harlow. "And I don't want to worry our children either."

My goal was to get his confession, but now that I had it, I didn't want it. "What's going on, Huntley?"

"Probably nothing—"

"Tell. Me."

"I know you." His blue eyes shifted back and forth between mine. "You'll insist on coming with me, but you're the only person I trust to protect Delacroix and our children in my absence or in the event of my demise."

I missed the days when it was just the two of us, when we could travel to the island and risk our lives for dragons, when we could fight Necrosis atop burning buildings. But now, we had responsibilities greater than the two of us. We had a kingdom to protect with our lives—and we had our babies. "Huntley…I need to know."

After a long stretch of silence, one spent testing the resolve in my eyes, he spoke. "Scouts spotted an unidentified black ship leaving our shores. Two yetis were slain in the valley halfway between the outpost and the Teeth without any other casualties."

I let that information soak in for a moment because it was a lot to take in. "What are you suggesting?"

"That there may be something going on with the Teeth right under our noses."

"Would they be that stupid after we granted them mercy?"

"We've taken their land and their source of food, so it's possible."

"Who was on the black ship?"

"I don't know," he said calmly. "There's not enough information to piece together a scenario, but I think it should be investigated. All the events could be unrelated. Perhaps that ship got lost and turned right back around after it made it to shore. Perhaps the people who killed the yetis were the Teeth themselves. Or perhaps someone came to our land to speak with the Teeth about an alliance."

My blood went cold at the thought.

"And perhaps they're plotting to overthrow the throne and take all the lands for themselves—including our people."

"How will you figure it out?"

"Ian and I will ask."

"You'll just show up on their doorstep and demand answers?" I asked incredulously.

"Not demand answers—but make threats."

"Just the two of you? You'll need an army."

"Dragons are more intimidating."

"Huntley, I don't like this."

"If they're plotting against us, they'll know I'm suspicious of them. And if they aren't plotting something, then they'll know I'll always anticipate their treason. A direct confrontation is the best tactic in this scenario. I'm not afraid of them—and they need to know that I won't hesitate to burn them all if I feel like it."

My arms remained crossed over my chest, the fear making my heart race. We'd enjoyed peace for so long, and I didn't want to revert to a time when I feared for my husband—and now my family.

He watched the emotions dance across my face. "I tried to avoid this."

"I needed to know."

"But our children don't, so this stays between us. They were raised in a very special time, a time when the world was a good place. They've never feared the loss of a parent or someone they love. They're adults now and should understand what freedom means since we worked so hard to earn it—but I'd prefer to keep them naïve as long as possible."

My arms remained locked over my chest like bars to a steel cage. I hadn't felt this kind of despair in so long that I didn't know how to digest it. "If we didn't have our children, I would go with you."

His eyes softened. "I know, baby."

"But I can't leave them…in case." My chin dropped, unable to confront the possibility that I could be a widow. A queen without her king.

"You can't leave our people either, Ivory. In the event I don't come back—"

"Please don't." I closed my eyes at the sting.

He paused a moment. "Delacroix and the Kingdoms will need you to lead them, to bring them victory just as we did in the past. There's no one else I would trust to do this except you. Not because you're my wife—but because you're my queen."

He always did this—made me fall in love with him all over again. "Please don't make me rule without you." Just the thought brought tears to my eyes. I could never look at the sky again if he weren't standing under it with me.

His hand moved to my cheek, and his thumb caught a tear the instant it fell. "I won't, baby."

Both of my hands gripped his wrists as I turned into his touch.

His thumb swiped across my bottom lip, and he looked at me the way he always did, like he might bend me over the desk and take me. "I love you, baby."

"I love you too."

His hand slid into my hair, and he brought me close, bending his neck so he could kiss me, catch my full lips with his authoritative mouth. He looked at me in a special way, like we were both blooming with youth and I was the most beautiful thing he'd ever seen. Some of the servant girls around the castle were beautiful and young, but I never saw him turn his head once. He still burned whenever he looked at me, the heat smoldering in his eyes like he wanted me then and there.

His arm moved across the small of my back, and he tugged me into him, his hand moving to its favorite spot—my ass. He squeezed it through my trousers as he backed me up to the couch in the sitting room.

My hands tugged at his clothes to get them off, to reveal his rock-hard body that could destroy mountains. His clothing fell to the floor, and mine came off and struck the rug like drops of rain. My back hit the cushions, and he was on top of me, his hips between my fleshy thighs before he was inside me with a firm thrust. His hand fisted in my hair, his stare so hard it looked angry. He fucked me like a whore but loved me like a queen.

His queen.

We fell asleep on the couch, a blanket from the back of the chair across our naked bodies. Huntley took up most of the space, so I had to cuddle so deep into him that we were practically one person—not that I minded. My leg was hiked over his hip, and our faces were pressed close together, just the way we were when we slept in our bed.

The door creaked, and then Harlow's voice came into the study. "Father?"

We both stilled when we heard her. We turned our heads to the door.

She didn't notice us right away, and when she did, she stilled in terror. Her eyes were so big, she looked like an owl rather than a person. The flush of her cheeks was instant, and she quickly fumbled backward to leave. "Uh…never mind." She closed the door behind her so hard it slammed.

"Remember when we didn't have kids?" I asked with a sigh.

"And we could fuck whenever and wherever we wanted? Yes, I remember." He tugged me close and pressed a kiss to my bare shoulder. "But she'll get over it. It's not like it's the first time."

I should get up and dressed, but I was so comfortable against his warm chest that I didn't want to leave. Huntley was busy most of the day and exhausted in the evenings, so we didn't have a lot of time to be together like this, to just coexist without something needing our attention.

"Keep an eye on Ethan. He might try something while I'm gone, and our daughter is too stubborn to be forthright with you."

"*Proud*," I said. "She's too *proud* to be forthright. And you know she gets that from you, right?"

"She gets everything from me."

"Now you know what I've put up with since the moment we met."

A subtle smirk moved on to his handsome face. "And we both know why you put up with it."

I gave him a playful smack in the shoulder. "Pig."

He pulled me close again and forced a kiss onto my lips.

I pretended to fight it, but I never wanted to fight anything from this man.

"We made a deal—and you better honor it going forward."

"What deal is this?"

He propped himself on his elbow and gave me a cold stare. "Ethan."

"It's not my fault he asked to speak to you."

"I told you I didn't want to deal with it." He sat up and left me behind, sitting in the corner of the couch with his foot propped on the coffee table. "You told me all I needed to do was respect her as an adult and stay out of her business. I did that—but I still had to deal with the bullshit." He looked at the fireplace once again, all moody.

I sat up and grabbed the clothing that had fallen in our heat. "Huntley." I pulled everything on, covering my naked body while he remained nude on the couch, not looking at me. "It's called being a father. You don't get to choose when being a father is most convenient for you."

His eyes remained on the fire, his jawline hard.

"She was just as uncomfortable as you were, so I'm sure she'll do everything she can to avoid that in the future. If Ethan hadn't pursued his own agenda, the circumstance wouldn't have happened in the first place, so it's not her fault."

"I never said it was."

"And I think you handled it well."

His eyes flicked back to mine, still hard but also surprised. "I wanted to cut his head off—"

"But you didn't."

"I almost exiled him from Delacroix—"

"*But you didn't.*"

His eyes narrowed in annoyance. "You have no idea how hard that was for me—"

"I do. And I think you did a wonderful job. Let's move on."

He looked at the fireplace again, his stare cold once more. "I'll try…"

8

HARLOW

I sat on the couch in my bedroom and read my book. I left the windows open so the summer breeze could move through my hair and bring the scent of jasmine to my nose. Sometimes, there was a gust of wind so strong it turned the pages in my book, but most of the time, it was gentle, relaxing.

I was supposed to go into town that evening to visit...*what was his name*? I realized I didn't even know it, that the man who had given me the best sex of my life didn't even have a name. I'd always been a sucker for the cocky bad boy, but I was also stubborn and refused to listen to orders, so I decided to blow him off.

Maybe he was the best sex of my life, but he didn't have any power over me. I was certain he was used to women bending over backward just for a moment of his attention, but I wasn't one of those girls. Never had been—and never would be.

I turned the page and then heard a quiet thud from across the room.

My eyes lifted from my book, expecting to see something on the floor because the breeze had knocked it over, but instead of *something,* it was *someone.* An arrogant smirk moved across his face when he caught me by surprise. "You think you can blow me off, baby?"

I froze on the couch, my fingers still pinching the page. My eyes glanced from him to the window, realizing he'd climbed up the castle walls to get to me. "Are you insane?" My fingers shut the hardback book with a dull snap, and I got to my feet. "You could have slipped and died."

He ignored what I said and drew close, his eyes turning heated as he regarded me in the tiny nightdress that barely covered anything. His fingers reached for the fabric at my waist and felt it between his fingertips before he gave a gentle tug, forcing my mouth toward his.

My body moved with the tug, but I turned my cheek to reject his kiss. "If someone saw you, my father will behead you—"

His hand gripped my chin with the speed of a striking snake and forced my eyes back on him. I tried to resist his hold, but it was like wiggling out of the embrace of a mountain. Those heated eyes watched me, like he didn't care about the risks or the danger. "I'm not scared of anyone, baby. Now get undressed."

"Someone will hear us—"

"Then be quiet."

"This is dangerous—"

"Like you've never had a guy up here."

My eyes narrowed at the accusation.

The asshole had the audacity to smile. "Act sweet and innocent all you want—it turns me on." He pushed down the tiny strap over my shoulder and let it fall, let one of my tits pop out, hard in the breeze that moved through the window. He gave it a squeeze before he pushed down the other strap. The material fell off my body immediately, leaving me to stand there in my panties.

He looked me up and down, like I was all his.

I felt my nipples harden into rocks, felt my heart race in excitement and fear.

His eyes lifted again and locked on mine. He studied me for a long time, as if he was reading the expression on my face like words on a page. "Are you afraid of me, baby?"

"I'm not afraid of anything."

"Ask me to leave—and I'll go."

"What about our deal?"

His eyes shifted back and forth between mine. "We can negotiate."

All I had to do was ask him to leave and he would return the way he'd come, but my lips remained tightly shut. "Then let's negotiate."

He reached behind his shoulders and pulled his shirt over his head, revealing the chiseled body that had made my toes curl several times. His biceps were plump with muscle, and all the different cuts of muscles along his arms and shoulders were so distinct they looked like they'd been marked with paint. A dark shadow was on his jawline, like he hadn't shaved since the last time we were together. It was another feature I liked on a man, feeling that stubble between my soft thighs.

He kicked off his boots and then dropped his trousers, stripping down until he stood in his underwear as I did. His hard chest was like a shield, and his stomach was solid like a plank of wood. A small trail of hair disappeared into his shorts. There was too much to look at it, and I found myself staring the way he had stared at me.

He backed me up to the foot of the bed, his arms by his sides, making me move with just his authority. When the backs of my knees hit the mattress, his large hands gripped my ass and lifted me, laying me on the bed before he tugged my ass to the edge. Then he lowered himself to his knees as his muscular arms scooped my legs and cradled them so I wouldn't have to hold them in position.

A flush of heat swept through me with a surge of fire. The excitement was potent, and I automatically bit my bottom lip when I realized what he was about to do—and I didn't even have to ask him.

He started with a simple kiss to the inside of one thigh and then the other. His kisses continued, and he gave me a gentle bite as he moved closer to where I wanted him most. Like he'd done this a lot, he built the anticipation before his lips finally arrived at mine, giving me a wet kiss with his warm mouth.

The moan I released was uncontrollable.

He kissed me again and again, moving slowly, making me desperate for more. It was a tease, and it was making me writhe harder on the bed, doing my best to keep my mouth shut, especially with the window still wide open.

Then his kisses turned hard, his full lips taking mine with purpose. His tongue swiped me, and he focused on the little nub that set my world on fire. He circled it with his tongue before he kissed me, before he sucked my lips into his mouth.

It felt so good I started to whimper. Whenever I gave head, I hoped to get it back in return. Most of the time, that didn't happen, and I never asked because that shattered my arousal. I wanted a guy to *want* to do it, not be asked to do it.

The whimpers turned to moans because it felt so damn good. My back arched, my hips pushed into his face, and I felt the scruff of his jaw scratch my thighs in the way I loved. My hand traveled down my stomach entirely on its own and dug into his hair, pushing him into my body because I wanted more.

He pulled his mouth away, and I wanted to scream in protest. His fingers flattened on my stomach before they moved up, sliding between my tits, and then up my neck. The shine on his lips was the dew of my arousal, and the sudden urge to kiss him swept over me. He grabbed my jaw and forced my lips apart to slide his thumb inside. "Suck."

I obeyed instantaneously, sucking his large thumb as he returned to his work between my legs. Now his kiss was demanding, borderline furious, an overload of kissing, sucking, and circling.

I knew why he'd slipped his thumb into my mouth—to shut me up.

When I wanted to moan, I sucked on his skin harder, both of my hands deep in his hair as I ground my body into his lips. "Fuck…" The word was lost on my tongue, absorbed by his thumb. Further and further, I inched, approaching the fireball of pleasure, writhing before it even hit.

It struck me like a blade against a shield, and I bit down on his thumb as I writhed in a hit of ecstasy even better than the previous ones he'd given me. My hips flexed on their own, and tears streaked from the corners of my eyes toward my ears. It was heaven. Goddamn heaven.

He kissed me until the uncontrollable writhing passed, until I stopped shoving my pussy into his face. He got to his feet and tugged down the front of his shorts to get his big-ass dick free before he shoved himself inside my soaked flesh, hitting my cervix with a single thrust. He released a quiet moan as he clenched his jaw, and it turned me on all over again.

He gripped the backs of my thighs and pinned them back as he thrust hard and fast, his face already tinted red from the arousal and exertion. It was a race to come, like pleasing me had been a pleasure rather than an obligation. He fucked me harder than he did last time, like he was so desperate to come that he couldn't slow down. Within a minute, he released, shoving his whole dick inside me as he stared down at me, ignoring the wince I made from his size.

He remained hard inside me, gently moving in and out through his own seed. His powerful chest rose and fell with his deep breaths, and blotches of red spread across his chest and stomach.

"How do you stay hard like that?"

His eyes moved to mine again before he tugged me closer, forcing his dick deep inside me again. "You." He fucked me hard, supporting my body so the headboard wouldn't tap against the wall. "It's all you, baby."

We dozed off in my bed, the bedroom window still open, the world quiet. The sky was a slight blue because the darkest part of the night had passed. In a couple hours, it would be dawn.

My eyes opened to the man beside me, who looked out of place in my champagne-pink bedding. His arm was hooked over my stomach but there was distance between us, so it wasn't a full cuddle like we'd had on the couch.

He seemed to know I was awake, because his eyes opened a second later. We stared at each other for a moment, and it was the first time I'd really had the opportunity to look deeply into his eyes, the color of warm coffee first thing in the morning.

"Tell me your name."

A slow smile crept on to his lips and reached his eyes. "Aurelias."

"I've never heard a name like that before."

"And I'm sure you'll never forget it."

"You ever get tired of being an asshole?" I challenged.

"Depends. Do you ever get tired of fucking one?"

My eyes narrowed on his face before I reached for the glass of water on my nightstand. "Want some water?"

"No."

My fingertips touched the glass and accidentally tipped it over. It fell to the rug and spilled everywhere, but the glass didn't shatter. My pitcher was empty because I'd drunk it before I started to read. "Well, there's that." I turned back to him.

His stare was suddenly cold, staring at where the glass had been a second ago.

"What's your problem?"

His eyes shifted to me, and that pissed-off expression lingered. "Someone could have heard that."

"I doubt it."

He lay back down again, this time releasing a heavy sigh. The energy from him was totally different now. His irritation was palpable. He ran his fingers through his hair as he stared up at the ceiling.

"It's getting late…or early, I guess. You should go."

"You can sleep in as long as you want."

"My father is departing at dawn, and I want to say goodbye. And you don't strike me as the kind of man that does sleepovers."

"I'm not." His arm moved behind his head, elongating the powerful muscles in his side. "Where's he going?"

"HeartHolme."

"What about your mother?"

"She'll stay with us." I turned my head to look at him. "Why do you care?"

His hard stare remained. "It means I can sneak in all I want since he won't be around."

"Uh, no," I said. "It doesn't mean that at all. And my mother has the wrath of a fire-breathing dragon."

A smile entered his features in amusement. "Don't pretend you don't want to do this again."

"I can do it with someone else."

"But it won't be as good—and we both know it." He continued to stare at me, the sexiest man who had ever been in this bed. "Just because I want to see you again doesn't mean I'm like Ethan. You wanted someone to fuck—and I'm that someone. So don't make it complicated with this bullshit."

"Bullshit?" I asked incredulously. "Not wanting you to sneak into my bedroom isn't bullshit."

"I wouldn't have had to if you'd kept your end of the bargain. And you're lucky I'm not making you keep the other part of the bargain too."

My eyes shifted away, thinking about what he really wanted to do to me.

"My place tomorrow after sunset." He stared at me, his eyes piercing and hard.

"That would be three nights in a row—"

"It's going to be *more* than three nights in a row."

I pushed the covers off and swung my legs over the edge.

His arm gripped my stomach, and he dragged me close, his lips burrowing into my neck with kisses, his big fingers digging into my body.

I tried to pry his arm off, but he gripped me tighter, pressed his kisses to my shoulder. My back flushed against his hard chest, and his scent smothered me. He was all man, all heat, and the second our bodies were close together, we were stuck like glue. I wanted this man more than any other—so I pushed him away as hard as I could.

He laid me back on the bed then moved on top of me. He grabbed my ankles and positioned my feet against his hard body, one against his stomach while the other was placed at the bottom of his chest.

He was hard like the cold ground in winter, and bumps moved across my skin when I felt that strength against my bare feet. His fingers reached for my neck and squeezed when he had me in place, gripping me like he owned me, when I'd only just learned his name. Then he pushed himself inside me and started to thrust, his thumb swiping up to my lips for me to suck.

I parted my mouth and took it, sucking his thumb hard to stifle the moans.

He fucked me hard again, his dick hard as the steel from my sword, and he reminded me why I would show up on his doorstep tomorrow night…and the night after that…and the night after that.

9

HARLOW

My father was armed to the teeth, wearing his full black armor that I'd never seen him wear in person. When we trained, he wore durable steel plates, but this was the stuff made for battle. His cloak was clasped behind, and it danced in the breeze behind him like a raised flag. He carried his sword on his hip and an axe across his back. Uncle Ian was dressed in the same way.

Something didn't feel right.

My mother was quiet, her eyes guarded against intrusion into her thoughts. She either looked at my father or out into the distance. I worried they would suspect I hadn't slept another night, but they were too distracted to notice.

That wasn't a good thing.

"Front or back?" Uncle Ian asked as he looked at Pyre.

Father gave him a cold stare.

"Front it is…" Uncle Ian kissed my mother goodbye then walked to the green dragon, giving us space to say farewell.

But it felt like goodbye.

My father directed a hard stare at my mother, arms by his sides, giving her a look he only ever gave her and no one else.

She stared back before she finally moved into his chest and kissed him goodbye. Not a quick peck on the lips kind of kiss, but a full-on, lovers type of kiss, and that made Atticus and me look at each other uncomfortably.

My father moved to Atticus next and gripped him by the shoulder. "Look after your mother while I'm gone." He cupped the back of his neck and kissed him on the temple. "Love you, son."

"Love you too, Father."

Father smiled with his eyes before he gave him a gentle pat on the cheek. Then he turned to me, and I noticed a distinct pause there, like saying goodbye to me was somehow harder. He took a breath and let it out before he drew close. "Take a walk with me."

My heart dropped into my stomach.

He led me away, walking across the grass until we were fully out of earshot.

"Something's going on…"

He faced me, his cloak billowing in the same summer breeze that had entered my bedroom window last night. "It's never easy to leave you."

"You've done it before—"

"But it's been a long time."

"You're wearing your battle armor, and you *never* wear that." I raised my voice, knowing we were isolated from everyone else. Frustrated tears never left my eyes, but they burned holes behind my sockets.

"It was your mother's request. She's overly cautious."

"What's there to be cautious of—"

"Harlow." He didn't raise his voice, but he deepened his tone to cut me off.

"It doesn't make any sense!"

"*Harlow.*"

I released a heavy breath, my nostrils flaring like an ox.

"I wanted a daughter who was smart and strong—and now I regret my wish." His blue eyes burned into mine, his authority as king ringing in the breeze around us. "A quality you've inherited from both of us, no doubt."

"Tell me what's really going on."

He regarded me in silence, his eyes still and focused, his mind deliberating. "You must keep it to yourself. Don't speak of it to your mother."

"But she already knows."

"It's easier to put on a brave face for others than yourself."

I inhaled a deep breath, the fear soaking into my skin and then the rest of my body.

"Uncle Ian and I need to investigate a disturbance at the bottom of the cliffs. We'll be armed with dragons and, therefore, untouchable. If my suspicions are correct, I'll issue a warning. And if they're wrong, I'll issue an apology. But it'll be nothing more than one or the other."

I tried to keep a straight face, but my deep breathing gave me away. "What suspicions—"

"The details don't matter."

"They do matter if I need to come get you."

Despite the edge in his eyes, a subtle grin appeared on his lips. "My job is to love you and protect you unconditionally—and your job is to allow me. Under no circumstances would I ever want you to risk your life for mine. When you have your own children, these words will resonate with you in a different way than they do now."

I gave a subtle shake of my head. "You're scaring me—"

"There's nothing to fear. I'll return within a week."

Now I avoided his gaze, my stomach in knots.

"Harlow."

I stared at the grass.

"Sweetheart."

My eyes shifted back to his.

"I'll be back before you know it."

"You promise?"

Silence stretched as he stared. "You're old enough to know I can't make that kind of promise."

"I don't like this—"

"In the event that I don't return and your mother is unfit to rule, chooses to step away, or…is no longer here…I've chosen you to succeed me."

"What?" All I cared about was his leaving, not receiving his crown. "What about Atticus?"

"You're my firstborn."

"I'm a woman—"

"A bullshit reason to be excluded from the title. I'm proud of the man Atticus has become, but you're the one who's meant to rule. I see myself in Atticus, but with you, we're identical."

"I couldn't do that to Atticus—"

"I've already spoken to him, and he's agreed that you're the better option."

"He did?"

"It's his kingdom too, Harlow. He wants the best for it—and that's you."

I couldn't picture myself running the Kingdoms the way my father did, with quiet authority, with the kind of respect he'd earned through a lifetime of dedication. He was the greatest hero in our history—and I just happened to be his daughter. "Father, I don't care about this right now. I just want you home."

"I know, sweetheart." His hand moved to my shoulder, and he squeezed it the way he did with Atticus. "I nearly gave my life for freedom, and I will give my life to keep it. That's my sacrifice—because this is the only world I ever want you to know." He released my shoulder and pulled me in for a hug, along with a kiss on the temple. "I'll do everything I can to make it back to you two and your mother—*always*."

We stared into the distance until Pyre was just a speck against the blue sky. Delacroix was now without a king, and the instant his presence was gone, the kingdom felt empty. My mother probably wanted to linger even longer, but she had to pretend she was unperturbed by his absence, so she returned to the castle.

I looked at my brother beside me. "The last thing I'd ever want is something to come between us."

He dragged his eyes from the horizon and looked at me.

"Our relationship means more to me than a crown."

To my surprise, the corner of his mouth quirked up in a smile, just the way Father's did. "You know I'm not a sore loser."

I felt the wind whip through my hair and sting my eyes. It was a windy day, but it was no deterrent for Pyre. "Are you sure this is okay?"

"Yes." He pivoted his body toward me, wearing the uniform that bore our family crest on the chest. He possessed features from both of our parents, was a perfect blend of the two. "Father and I both agreed that Delacroix needs your leadership and my sword. I'm more suited to serve, to fight for our people, and I would gladly serve you, Harlow."

Somehow, my brother's confidence meant more than my own father's. "Really?"

He gave a slight nod. "Really."

"I thought Father would select you, since the general of Delacroix is the more obvious choice."

"I'm not the general yet. Father says it's a title I still need to earn. And I can't do both, Harlow. The Queen of Delacroix needs to rule over our people, and the general of Delacroix needs to rule over the army. They're two different kingdoms in the same place."

"You think I'd be a good queen?"

His eyes studied me as that smile slowly returned to his face. "Absolutely."

"But you're always saying how annoying I am—"

"You are annoying."

"And that I'm stupid—"

"I didn't say you *are* stupid. I said you *act* stupid."

"And you think I would be a good queen?" I asked in disbelief.

"When you aren't being stupid and annoying, yes, I think you're pretty great. But I wouldn't worry about it too much because Mother and Father will be around for a long time. Father is in better shape than I am, and he's decades older. And Mother is as sharp as a tack. You don't have to worry about this for a long time, Harlow."

My heart tightened like a clenched fist, carrying the heavy burden of the truth. But I kept it to myself, held that secret in the pit of my stomach. My eyes moved back to the blue sky, no longer able to see the mighty dragon that carried my father upon his back. "Yeah… you're right."

"You seem down." Brianna sat beside me at the bar, both of us with tankards of beer.

My eyes flicked back up to hers. "My father left this morning." This wasn't news that should be shared with the public, but I knew I could tell her.

"Doesn't he visit HeartHolme often?"

"Yes, sometimes."

"Then why are you worried?"

I shrugged. "You know me, I always worry."

"Uh, no," she said. "You never worry."

I covered the tightness of my face by taking a drink. "So, what happened with Ethan?"

"What happened with Ethan?" she asked incredulously. "I want to hear about Hot Motherfucker. Now, that sounds like an erotic adventure."

I gave a quiet chuckle. "You go first."

"Well, you were right, Ethan is good in bed."

"You're welcome." I clanked my glass against hers.

"But afterward, he was all weird."

"Weird how?"

"Really cold, standoffish, hostile…threw a fist into the wall…and then I think he kinda cried a bit?"

"Uh, what do you mean cried a bit?"

"His eyes were wet and red, like he was about to cry."

I was horrified, but I did my best not to show it.

"He's not over you."

It had been just last week when he'd asked my father's permission to marry me. I'd found his intensity attractive when I met him, but now, it felt like too much.

"So, does Hot Motherfucker have a name?"

I pulled my gaze away from my tankard and looked at her once more. "Aurelias."

"Ooh…exotic."

"I didn't know his name until last night."

"That's hot."

"I'm supposed to go over there tonight, but…"

"But what?"

"I feel like I'm walking into another Ethan situation."

"He's clingy?"

"No."

"Then I don't understand."

"I'm afraid I'm the one who will become clingy."

"Ooooh."

"He's got this 'I don't give a fuck about anything or anyone' kind of attitude that just drives me crazy. I want to make him give a fuck. And he's so beautiful. His eyes are like chocolate and coffee, and he's so hard…like harder than this countertop." I smacked the surface with my palm.

"Like…his dick is that hard?"

"No," I said with a laugh. "His chest, his shoulders…"

She gave a sigh. "He sounds dreamy."

"And he's so good in bed. Like, hot damn." I took another drink.

"Do you only want him because you can't have him, or do you actually want him? Because that's how you are. You like the chase. It was that way with Ethan."

"I'm not sure." I put my walls up high from the beginning, afraid to show any kind of vulnerability whatsoever. I was normally confident, but he made me uneasy, made me nervous, made me afraid of pain the second our eyes met. "He's the hottest guy I've ever been with. No comparison. I'm just waiting for him to ghost me…"

"You forget how hot you are, Harlow."

I stuck out my tongue and blew.

"Oh, shut up. You know you're hot, Harlow."

"Yes, I'm easy on the eyes, but this man is pure fire. No comparison."

"Well, I disagree."

I finished my tankard and set it on the bar. "Well, do you think you'll see Ethan again?" My eyes took a quick scan of the bar, seeing all the villagers enjoying their pints after a long day in the fields and the shops. My eyes scanned over someone I recognized, but it took me a second to react.

"I don't know. The sex was good, but the aftermath kinda sucked."

My eyes locked on his, eyes that I used to stare into most nights. We would hide away in the loft above his studio, the winter chill frosting the corners of the window. His body used to keep me warm, and the fire in his eyes used to burn me.

Brianna noticed my distraction and followed my gaze, watching Ethan sit alone in the corner, staring me down. "Well, this is awkward."

I broke contact first and looked away.

"I think he wants to talk to you. Maybe sleeping with him was a bad idea." She finished the rest of her drink and left her empty tankard next to mine. "I'll let you two chat." She walked out of the bar, leaving the stool empty beside me.

Ethan crossed the bar, dressed in all black, and took the stool next to me. Muscles stretched the fabric of his shirt. His pretty eyes were hollow with loss. His intensity was always profound, one of the reasons I'd wanted him in the first place. Now he stared, anger and sadness swirling together like a hurricane in his eyes. "I'm dying inside, and you're perfectly fine."

"Well, you fucked my friend—"

"And you don't care. At all."

"Ethan—"

"Harlow." His tone deepened. "You're just going to throw this away?"

"Ethan—"

"I fucking love you—"

"Stop." I held up my hand because I didn't want to hear another declaration. "My father threatened to kill you if you bothered me again."

"And he's not here, is he?"

"But when he comes back—"

"I'll deal with it then."

He was so lucky that I wouldn't rat him out to my father.

"I've seen you sneak into the castle late at night." His eyes questioned me with their hostility, searching for the answer he already had.

I stayed quiet, refusing to answer the question he wouldn't ask. "You want me to tell you the honest truth, Ethan?"

"Yes."

"It'll hurt."

He stilled, his breathing slightly deeper. "I want to know."

"I always knew you weren't going to be my husband." I yanked the gauze off the wound, and now everything was exposed to the cold air. I felt the sting of my words, and I knew he felt it too.

He gave no reaction, but I knew he was hurt. "If that's true, why did you stay so long?"

"Because it was fun and easy. I didn't want the relationship to end, but I knew we didn't have a future."

"I could be your husband if you gave me a chance—"

"It's one of those things that you just know. Whatever you're supposed to feel when you fall in love...I've never felt that. Ethan, you're such a great guy, and you deserve a woman who wants you with the same intensity as you want her. Would you really want to be with me if you had to talk me into it?"

His stare continued.

"You deserve better than that, Ethan."

"Maybe that's true, but you're the only woman who's made me feel this way. What I feel when I make all my pieces...is how I feel every time I look at you."

It was like a punch to the stomach.

"Yes, I deserve better, but I'd be willing to be patient with you."

Now that punch turned into a knife. "Ethan, I'm sorry—"

"Hey, baby." Aurelias appeared out of nowhere, standing directly beside us, the tallest, hottest, sexiest guy in the room by a long shot. His hand immediately moved into my hair, and he leaned down and kissed me.

It all happened so fast, I didn't react.

Aurelias looked at Ethan, a silent showdown happening with his cold gaze.

Ethan stared back, his features hard and impossible to decipher.

I wished I were somewhere far, far away.

Ethan finally stood up. "Hope you find what you're looking for, Harlow." He walked out of the bar and stepped into the night. The door swung closed behind him.

Aurelias took his vacated seat, tapped his fingers on the bar and was immediately served. Instead of getting a beer, he got scotch because their inventory had been restocked. As if nothing had happened, he just sat there, his elbow on the counter, his fingers against the scruff of his hard jawline.

"That was a dick move."

He took a drink before he looked at me. "I just did you a favor."

"No, you were just being a dick—"

"If you want to set the guy free, you've got to break him. Destroy any chance of hope. Hurt him so much that he hates you, because it's easier to hate someone than love them when they don't love you back."

He'd basically just told me he'd broken a lot of hearts without an ounce of guilt. He made women fall in love with him and then made them watch him walk out with another woman on his arm. "It sounds like you speak from experience."

"I make my intentions and expectations very clear."

"Have you ever been in love?"

His eyes were cold, like I'd insulted him. "Have you?"

"No."

"Let's get out of here."

"You didn't answer my question."

"You already know the answer."

10

AURELIAS

The second the door was closed, I pushed her up against it and slid my hands underneath her top, reaching her silky bra and the plump tits underneath. I squeezed them both in my big hands as I kissed her, rock hard at the feel of her gorgeous body. She was petite, over a foot shorter than me, but she was all woman. She had muscles in her arms and legs, a flat stomach with her core muscles distinct, an ass that was plump like a nectarine. Whenever my body made contact with hers, I was swept away in the throes of passion, and I knew she was too.

Her body simmered like a pot of boiling water. The heat was in her core, in the center between her legs, in the tips of her fingers. She burned like a fireplace in the midst of winter, smoldering with heat and smoke. And she burned hotter and hotter the longer I kissed her, and I knew just how wet she was becoming with every passing second.

I undid my trousers and yanked them open, dragging them down until my cock and balls were free. "On your knees."

She obeyed with enthusiasm, slipping her hands underneath my shirt to grip my torso as she drew my length into her mouth.

I pulled off my shirt then dug my fingers into her hair, excited to feel her mouth sheathe my dick to the base. She fucked good, so I'd suspected she sucked good too.

She kissed my head the way she kissed my mouth before she swiped her tongue to taste me. Her eyes lifted to mine as she opened her mouth wide and took me, pushed my length as far as she could take it. Then her fingers cupped my balls and massaged them as she sucked my dick like it was a great honor.

My hand fisted her hair, and I watched her, thrusting my hips slightly to push my dick into her mouth, to push it farther than she wanted to take it. It didn't take long for her lips to turn plump with irritation from all the sucking and friction.

I could feel the burn inside her chest, between her legs. The heat rivaled the warmth of her mouth. She was the one on her bare knees on the hardwood floor, but she enjoyed it as much as I did. "You like that big dick in your mouth, baby?" I gripped her neck and thrust harder, forcing my way in and giving her little time to breathe.

Tears pooled in her eyes, and her flames burned hotter.

I could hold my load until the most opportune time, but her enthusiasm tested my willpower. I was the one who had to stop it, because if I didn't, the fun would end too soon. We moved to the couch, all our clothes on the floor, and before I could push her down onto the cushions, she pushed me into the back of the couch.

Her little body climbed on top of mine, straddling my hips, her hands pressing against my hard chest as she got into position. "You're so fucking hot…" Her eyes looked down over my body, all the hardness and the grooves between the muscles.

I grabbed my base and directed myself to her lower lips, finding the slit like my dick had its own sight.

She lowered herself, sheathing my dick as far as she could before the wince kicked in. Her nails clawed at my shoulders before she moved up and down, rocking her hips at the same time, taking my dick over and over with a flutter in her chest.

I closed my eyes briefly, because it just felt that good. She wasn't just wet and tight, but her warmth and stickiness were mind-blowing. I'd fucked a lot of pussy, but hers was something special.

Her pleasure was like repeated tidal waves, one after another, her desire so hot it scorched me. She got off on my size, but she also got off on how good she made me feel. She couldn't feel my thoughts the way I could feel hers, but she could feel just how hard she made me. She could see it written all over my face.

My hands gripped her sexy hips, and I lifted her up and down with my strength, relieving her exertion so she could keep going without stopping. Her tits were in my face, her nipples hard, her brown hair cascading around her shoulders.

I wanted to come right then and there.

I finally felt the distant burn between her legs, the sensation that was unique to each woman because they all came differently. Some felt it in their extremities first. Some felt it deep in their core. The durations were different too. Harlow's were gradual in the beginning and intense at the end. It was a slow burn, traveling from her core to the area between her legs, flames that rose as high as buildings. It came closer and closer, making her eyes flutter and her lips part.

Feeling an orgasm that wasn't my own made it so hard not to come. That was why I couldn't last long after she was finished, because making and feeling a woman come was the sexiest thing ever.

My thumb moved to her clit and rubbed it gently, wanting to give her that extra push into oblivion. The second she felt my touch, her hips bucked and then the rest of her reactions fell into place. A fire that burned hotter than the sun unleashed, and the cataclysm of pleasure radiated throughout her whole body. Her blue eyes glistened with tears before the drops slipped down her cheeks. The moans she made sounded like roars. She rode a high that was higher than the clouds, a pleasure so intense that it broke my resolve.

I came with a grunt, filling that pussy with my sterile seed, writhing in her pleasure as well as my own. We came in unison, our hips moving together, our hands gripping each other for balance.

It felt better than the last time, but I had that thought every time I fucked her. Every woman had different emotions, but Harlow's were different. They were constantly at the surface, just below her skin, like she could snap in rage or exult in joy in a split second.

I rolled her to her back against the couch and positioned myself at the deepest angle I could get, spreading her legs and hooking one over my shoulder. She'd sucked me good and then fucked me good.

Now it was time I returned the favor.

She crashed on the couch afterward and pulled a blanket over her naked body to stay warm. I set the glass of water directly in front of her, so it would be the first thing she saw when she woke up. With her father outside the kingdom, the timing couldn't be better. I could transfer her while she was half asleep and slip out of Delacroix without anyone noticing. Her family wouldn't know she was missing until late morning, and without her father there to lead the search, the queen wouldn't know what to do.

I left my bag against the wall by the door, along with my sword. I was dressed in my armor, ready to go the second she took that drink to take advantage of every second of its duration.

A very small part of me felt like shit for what I was about to do, but it wasn't enough to stop me. Harlow shouldn't drop her guard in front of strangers, shouldn't sleep with a man without even knowing his name. She might be skilled with the blade, but she lacked the awareness of someone of her birth.

I stood at the counter and looked over the maps Rancor had given to me. Once King Rolfe had come into power, he'd removed the barrier between the top and bottom of the cliffs. Instead of a secret passage carved out of rock, a path was now built into the side of the cliff face. It was wide enough for horses and wagons, for shipments between Delacroix and Heart-Holme. It was the path I'd taken here, and I would have to take it on the return route in the middle of the night to avoid others on the road. Once I was at the bottom, I would have to get her across the snow to their domain—and avoid yetis along the way. She would be combative, so drugging her would be my only option for cooperation, but if I drugged her too much, I could kill her—and then she would be useless.

A sensation pressed against me...a sense of alarm. My chin lifted to see Harlow across the room near the door, fully dressed like she wanted to slip out without a word. She did it silently, like she hoped I was upstairs and would escape without my notice.

My eyes glanced at the water I'd left on the coffee table—and it remained untouched.

My alarm deepened as she regarded the sword, and then a jolt of terror erupted through her.

I abandoned the map and came around the counter, doing my best to be quiet and try to sneak up on her.

But she turned when my boot made the floorboard creak. Those confident eyes were still with hostility. She quickly took in my appearance, seeing the traveling clothes and the armor that no other kingdom bore.

She was smart—too smart—and tried to pretend nothing was wrong even though her insides screamed.

"This is a nice sword… I've never seen these kinds of markings before." She referred to the snake print along the scabbard, the hint of gold in the creases. It was unlike their human swords, different in every way even though they had the same purpose.

I came closer.

She locked her eyes with mine, waiting for a moment to run or fight. The adrenaline pumped in her ears. Terror washed over her, along with self-loathing. "You have nothing to say?"

I knew what she was doing. The mind couldn't focus on two things at once, so if I spoke, my reflexes wouldn't be quite as strong, so it would be her opening to run or attack. "It's nothing personal—"

She grabbed a wine bottle and chucked it at my head.

I sidestepped it and rushed her.

She dodged out of the way of the sword and grabbed the first thing she could reach, a book sitting on a table. She threw that at me too on her way to finding something more formidable. She probably would have reached for the sword instead, but I intentionally blocked her way. When she made it to the kitchen, she shattered the base of an empty bottle and used that as a weapon, facing me with blood lust in her eyes.

I faced her, giving a sigh of irritation. "Don't make me hurt you."

"Who are you?"

"I told you my name—"

"Then *what* are you?"

"Just because I have a sword doesn't make me a bad guy—"

"A banker doesn't have a sword—let alone a sword like *that*. I've never seen anything like it in all my years, meaning it wasn't made in the Kingdoms or Heart-Holme. And your clothing has the crest of a snake—a symbol I've never seen used. My father left because danger lurks across our lands, and now I realize *you're* the danger. Now answer me. *What* are you?"

Harlow was a lot smarter than I'd given her credit for. "I meant what I said. I have no desire to hurt you—"

"We're both going to bleed before this is over." She lunged at me, slicing the jagged bottle toward my face, moving as fast as I'd seen her move when she trained with her father. When I tried to grab her, I missed, and she sliced the bottle down toward my arm. She made me bleed like she'd said she would, but my armor protected me from most of it. "I'm going to kill you and hang you right above the castle doors."

"Spoken like a king."

She lunged at me again.

This time, I grabbed her wrist and spun her around, forcing the bottle out of her hand and onto the floor. I kicked it away so she wouldn't accidentally step on it then tightened my arm across her neck, cutting off her air supply so she would struggle to breathe. My hold on her body was so strong that her kicks were useless, and she eventually gave up, going limp in my arms.

I gently lowered her to the floor then picked up the bottle from where it'd been kicked into the other room. Then I heard the sound of steel leaving a scabbard and turned back around to see Harlow standing there, holding my sword by the hilt, murder in her eyes.

Despite her small size, she spun the sword around her wrist like it was made for her even though it had been crafted in another world far away from this one. There was an arrogant smirk on her lips too, like no amount of good sex would dampen her resolve now. She would strike me down and kill me. "Run."

"I don't run, sweetheart." A smirk moved on to my lips as I stared at her. All I should have felt was annoyance that she'd tricked me, but I felt a surge of admiration instead. I tossed the bottle aside because I could kill her by mistake if I weren't careful.

We stared each other down in the open space between the entryway and the living room, her holding the heavy sword with ease, like a lifetime of training had prepared her wrists and forearms to bear the weight. The adrenaline in her heart was probably giving her an extra push as well.

Then she moved, spinning the blade for my neck to end my life quickly.

I dodged out of the way and avoided another strike that would have cut at the armor on my torso.

She chased me around the house, slicing into the furniture and knocking over dressers as she went.

I was much faster than her, despite her proficiency with the blade, and that was something she could never replicate as a human.

She groaned in frustration, unable to land a single blow. "How are you doing this?"

I came at her and blocked her blade perfectly with my vambrace and forced the blade down to the floor. I slammed her wrist into my knee and forced her to drop the blade before I moved to grab her again.

This time, she punched me right in the face and threw an upper hook at my jaw. She wasn't big enough to knock me out, but it still made my mouth flood with blood. This was a battle she couldn't possibly win, but I admired her for how well she put up a fight. I spun her arm around mine, kicked her in the back of the knee and forced her to drop, and then locked my arm across her neck again. I cut off her air supply and watched her struggle against my hold. "I'll make sure you don't fake it this time."

11

HUNTLEY

It was a full day's ride to HeartHolme, and we touched down at dusk. I'd grown up in the cold, so it had no effect on me as a man, but it still caught me by surprise when I felt it after the warmth of Delacroix. When we landed, I gave Pyre a pat on the snout then entered the city with my brother, remembering the battle that had nearly claimed the front gate. It was there that I defeated Haldor, one of the Three Kings who almost ended my mother's life.

We walked through the city, the torches already aglow down the cobblestone pathways and the alleys between buildings. It hadn't changed in these last few decades, but the inhabitants flourished without fear of Necrosis and the Teeth.

"Let's rest for the night before we provoke the Teeth," Ian said. "I'd prefer to visit them in daylight anyway."

I expected Avice and Lila to be waiting for him at the gate after Pyre was spotted from the sky by the scouts, and when they weren't there, I expected to intercept them on our way to the castle, but that hadn't happened either. "I should speak with Mother. She hasn't seen me in a while."

"And she would never forgive you if you didn't visit her first," he said with a slight grin.

We finally reached the castle and entered the double doors, swallowed by the warmth from the stone fireplace. The furniture hadn't been updated in over twenty years, but it was free of dust and cobwebs since the servants were diligent in their upkeep.

We moved up the stairs, heading to the top where Mother's quarters were positioned.

"Where's your family?"

Ian remained ahead, leading the way like I'd forgotten every path I'd trod hundreds of times. "I'm sure we'll see them soon enough."

We made it to the landing, checked in with her guards, and then stepped into her private chambers that had a remarkable view of the city and beyond. My mother rose from her chair the second we entered the room, her eyes locked on mine like Ian wasn't there. She wore her uniform with the family crest, her coat made of feathers that matched the ones woven into her hair.

Time had disrupted the details of her appearance, like the skin around her eyes and mouth, and the strength of her posture, but she was still the same queen she'd always been, her sword still on her hip like war could appear at her borders at any moment. Her eyes lit up with the unconditional affection she'd shown me over a lifetime, and then the smile that moved on to her lips reminded me of the way I looked at my own son and daughter.

"My son." She stepped closer to me and circled my body with her arms, squeezing as tight as her frail body could.

I returned the embrace, wrapping her body in my arms, my chin resting on her head. "I've missed you, Mother."

"Oh, not as much as I've missed you." She pulled away and cupped both of my cheeks like I was still a boy. "How's your family?"

"They're well."

Ian excused himself. "I'll let you guys catch up. Huntley, I'll meet you at our usual spot." He walked out, and the guard closed the door behind him.

"Take a seat, son." She gestured to her servant, who fetched me a drink after my long journey.

I sat in the other armchair, directly across from my mother, watching her look at me like I was her pride and joy. "How are you?"

"My eyes are tired. My bones are tired. But my heart is relentless."

"Ian thinks you're immortal."

She smiled. "I just have too much to live for."

"I hope he's right."

"Don't despair, Huntley. We still have so much time left. How's Harlow?"

"I told her she would be queen someday. She seemed surprised."

"Because she's not an arrogant brat. She has your brains and her mother's humility."

"And her beauty."

She gave a slight nod. "She does."

"We've officially reached the age where I have to acknowledge that my daughter is a woman."

Her hands rested on the armrests, curling forward slightly. "She has a man in her life?"

"She did. He asked to marry her—but she said no."

"I'm sure a lot of men want to marry her."

"And I want no part in it."

She gave me a pitiful smile. "You always told me you would raise your daughters like your sons."

"And I have."

"Not in this category. You don't care about Atticus's personal life. You shouldn't be disturbed by hers."

"Easier said than done."

"Did I ever interfere in yours?"

I directed my gaze on her and gave her a cold stare.

"Oh, that's right…I did."

My glare softened into a partial smile.

"But that was different," she said. "How's Atticus?"

"He's a good man. I'm proud to call him my son."

"But you seem more invested in Harlow."

"I don't have a favorite."

"All parents have a favorite, Huntley. And we both know which son is mine."

I held her gaze. "I love my children equally. The only reason I'm more invested in Harlow is because she looks like my wife…and I love my wife deeply. I would protect her with my life, so it's hard not to feel that way toward Harlow. You succeed as a parent when your children no longer need you, but it's hard to imagine a time when my little girl doesn't need me anymore."

"She doesn't need you now, Huntley. If you've selected her for the crown, that means you believe she can not only take care of herself, but all the Kingdoms. It's the greatest compliment you could give her."

I looked out the window, seeing the darkness and the torches beyond. "What happened between Ian and Avice?" I turned back to her to meet her gaze. "My wife would be running into my arms the second I returned from my travels. I've seen no sign of his wife or his daughter since we've set foot in HeartHolme."

My mother stared at me for a long time, treating the conversation with the formality of diplomacy. "They've been separated awhile now."

I didn't react, but I felt the tightness between my ribs. I treated Avice with the same affection that Ian treated Ivory, welcoming her as a sister rather than an in-law, but the pain came on my brother's behalf. I knew how much he loved her, and whatever the reason for their separation, it broke him.

"She's asked for a divorce more than once."

"And you've denied it?"

"I told her I would consider it, but I'm only stalling to give Ian a chance to make this right."

"So, he's in the wrong?"

My mother held my stare. "This is his tale, not mine."

I joined him at the pub, sitting in the chair across from him at a table in the corner. I wore my heavy coat on top of my armor, back to the old attire of my youth, when I'd fallen in love with the woman who would become my wife.

He already had a beer ready for me. "They have pot roast tonight."

"Haven't had that in a long time."

"I ordered two."

"Could use something warm."

We drank our beer and sat in silence for a while. Ian was tense, his eyes on his beer or out the window, as if he dreaded the question that he knew was coming. When I didn't ask, he moved on. "Did you tell her about Harlow?"

"Yes. She told me to treat Harlow the way I treat Atticus."

"Easier said than done."

"Has Lila had any suitors?"

"None that I know of."

The barmaiden brought the pot roast with a loaf of bread to share. Her eyes lingered on mine, knowing exactly who I was before she retreated to the bar to serve the other patrons.

With our elbows on the table, we ate without manners, our wives not there to patrol our dinner behavior.

When he didn't mention it himself, I went for it. "You can tell me, or I can ask. How do you want to play this?" Ian and I didn't have deep conversations about anything. I never shared the details of my relationship with Ivory. He knew me better than most people, but he still didn't know the depth of my thoughts, not like my wife did.

He dipped his bread in the stew, soaking it until he popped it into his mouth.

"Alright, then." I abandoned my food and stared at him. "What happened?"

Ian still didn't say anything, like he wasn't ready to talk about it. "Mother tell you?"

"I figured it out the moment we got here." Ivory would never treat me with indifference, would never disrespect me like that. It was as if Avice didn't care whether Ian lived or died. She probably didn't even know he'd left. "I asked her for details, but she protected your privacy."

"I thought you were the favorite."

"Even if I were, she's still loyal to you."

He continued to eat, drawing it out as long as possible. There was barely any stew left in his bowl, but he continued to soak it up with his bread, just for something to do. "We've been separated awhile."

"Why?"

"Because I fucked up, Huntley." Once the words were out, he pushed his food aside, as if the truth destroyed his appetite.

I felt the pity enter my gaze when he probably didn't deserve it. "Don't stick your dick in other women. It's not hard, Ian."

"It's a lot more complicated than that—"

"It's not." I would never violate my commitment to my wife. There were offers when she wasn't looking, from the maidens in the castle to women my daughter's age in the bar. Never once was I tempted.

Ian looked out the window, the cold appearing as frost in the corners. "A few months ago, she found out she was pregnant…"

My eyes narrowed because I hadn't anticipated a tale like this.

"It was unplanned, obviously. We tried to give Lila a sibling for a very long time, and it was hard on Avice when we couldn't. She assumed it was her fault, no matter how many times I told her I could be the problem, not her. So, when she found out she was pregnant, she was overjoyed…and I wasn't."

I listened to my brother, my eyes on his face while he continued to stare out the window.

"The kid would be twenty years younger than Lila, so that's not much of a sibling. Plus, at Avice's age…you know."

I gave a nod in understanding.

"I suggested we terminate it…and that upset her. She wanted another baby so much that she couldn't think clearly. She couldn't consider all the risk factors, the fact that this didn't really benefit Lila, because if we both died, Lila would be the one raising it in our place when that shouldn't be her responsibility."

I would have known if Ian had another child, so I already knew how this story would end.

"She didn't make it past the first month..." Ian finally turned his gaze back to me, able to look me in the eye again. "And she was devastated. She started to resent me because she assumed I asked the gods for this to happen, when I would never do such a thing. Her depression deepened. She pulled away from me. This went on for months. I started to resent her, because before she became pregnant, our lives were perfect. It was shattered because she let her emotion cloud her judgment. So, at my lowest point, I did something I shouldn't have..."

My judgment faded once I realized the emotional intensity of the situation. "She caught you?"

"I told her—and it was the final nail in the coffin."

"Why did you do it?"

"When you go months without your wife even looking at you...it's nice to feel wanted. And a lot of women want me, all the time. There've always been offers left and right when she's not around, but I've never cared. I guess a part of me hoped it would make her realize how far apart we would drift if she didn't let me in again...and that she might lose me. But it had the opposite consequence."

I couldn't verbalize my pity. I couldn't comfort his sadness. It was one of those rare times when I had no idea what to say. It was a lot to digest. "I wish you had confided in me when this was happening."

"I didn't want to talk about it."

"I could have helped you."

"You don't understand how delirious Avice was. No one could help her." He looked away again. "And to make matters worse..." There was a pause, a heavy one, a shine in his eyes that was quickly blinked away. "My daughter hates me." He forced his voice to remain steady, to mask the crack that wanted to escape. "She knows what I did and wants nothing to do with me."

The pain transferred from his body to mine, a burn that consumed my veins, flesh, and bones. It was every parent's worst nightmare, to dedicate your life to your child, only to watch them despise you. "Avice shouldn't have told her that."

"She overheard us talking." His gaze was glued to a spot on the window, like focusing on a single point was all he could do to keep his composure. "I haven't been with anyone else since, even though she's made it clear we're no longer together and I'm free to do what I want."

"Have you been pursuing her?"

"I gave up on that."

"Ian, you can't give up—"

"Don't oversimplify something complicated."

"I'm not. But you have no other choice but to try…if you want to stay married."

Ian grabbed his mug and took a drink, finishing the contents and shaking it until every last drop was in his mouth.

"I'll talk to her."

"Good luck with that."

Now I wished Ivory were with me, because she was much better at this sort of thing. Or Harlow. She was exceptional at this stuff.

"I've always been the lesser brother…in every way imaginable."

"That's not true, Ian."

"This wouldn't happen with you."

"I admit I wouldn't have fucked someone else, but this situation could have easily happened to me. Ivory and I have been through our fair share of marital strain. It wasn't easy, but we got through it. If you still love her—"

"Of course I still fucking love her," he snapped. "My life was perfect until this shit happened. Lila and I were close. And then the fucking gods decided to smite me. Now I don't have a family."

"*Ian.*" I looked him dead in the eye. "You always have a family."

He looked away. "It's not the same thing."

"We're blood. My children are your blood. And your daughter will always be your blood."

He continued to look out the window.

"I'll talk to her."

"That's not going to do anything—"

"We're not going to stop until we fix this, Ian. I'm with you on this."

"Huntley, I slept with someone else—"

"And while that was the wrong decision, this is a complicated situation, and you wouldn't have done that otherwise. It's all about the context."

"Rancor is more important right now."

"Nothing is more important than family," I said. "The Teeth will face our wrath tomorrow."

Avice had left her accommodations in the castle and moved in to the village. Lila had done the same, having her own home nearby. I approached the door and knocked, the torch outside flickering in the subtle breeze. It'd been our intention to implement electricity in HeartHolme after the war, but it was such a grand undertaking that it never happened. Homes were still warmed by fireplaces, and the streets were lit by flames. My mother was also too proud to change things, afraid it would soften her people who thrived in the snow.

The Forsaken Vampire

The door opened, and Avice faced me, her brown hair pulled back in a braid. Her eyes were empty at the sight of me. I'd done nothing to her, but she regarded me as a stranger rather than her brother-in-law, rather than her sovereign. Her hand remained on the door as she stared at me.

I stared back. "We have a lot to catch up on."

"I think you're already caught up, Huntley."

"Are you going to invite me inside?"

Her eyes flashed back and forth between mine, her hand still on the door to bar my entry.

"Or am I going to have to force my way inside?"

"I don't want to talk about it—"

"As King of All Kingdoms, I order you to step aside."

"You're really going to play that card?" she asked coldly.

"Absolutely."

She finally released the door and moved inside the house, the fireplace burning and illuminating the entire sitting room. White candles burned on the table and the counter, casting a light that reached the deepest corners.

I removed my coat and hung it on the coatrack.

She stood there, arms crossed over her chest, her eyes guarded.

"Ian told me everything that happened. So first of all, I want to tell you how sorry I am that you lost your child. I never told Ian this, but Ivory and I went through the same thing after we had Harlow and Atticus. It wasn't easy for either of us, but especially her."

Her walls crumbled slightly, the softness reaching her eyes and mouth. "I'm sorry to hear that."

"I know you are. And I know you understand the pain. But you have a wonderful daughter, and I have my children. I consider us lucky."

She gave a slight nod, but her arms remained crossed over her chest. "Would you like something to drink?"

"Scotch—if you have it."

The corner of her mouth ticked in a smile. "Men never change." She moved into the kitchen and made herself a tea and returned with my drink. We took a seat at the dining table, facing each other as the fire burned in the hearth. We sat for a while, neither one of us saying anything.

"Why are you in HeartHolme?"

"Ian and I have to take care of something."

"I assume Ivory isn't here. Otherwise, she'd be the one having this conversation."

I nodded. "I wish I'd known about you and Ian sooner."

"I'm surprised he didn't tell you."

"As am I."

She sank in the chair, arms still crossed over her chest. "When I was Necrosis, I knew I couldn't have children, something I wanted more than anything. And then I was given a second chance, and Ian and I had a beautiful daughter. When we couldn't have another, I was heartbroken, even though I reminded myself to be grateful rather than greedy. Our second baby came twenty years too late, but it was still a blessing, nonetheless. The loss was unbearable…" Her eyes shone in the light of the candles, a distinct gloss. She quickly blinked it away. "I knew Ian didn't want it, and I fear he prayed to the gods for a different outcome."

"He didn't."

"We'll never know—"

"My brother would never do that, Avice. I know he's broken your trust, but he's not a liar, and he's proven that he's not a liar. He's a man of honesty and integrity. Otherwise, he wouldn't have told you what he'd done."

She watched me, her eyes guarded once again.

"Ian fucked up. No argument there. But you know how much he loves you. You know this isn't something he would do in any other circumstance. Ian could have cheated all throughout your marriage without getting caught, but he never has. Please give him another chance."

"Can I ask you something, Huntley?"

I felt my muscles stiffen.

"If you went through a depression so deep that you couldn't get out of bed, and Ivory slept with someone else, would you forgive her?"

I couldn't picture that, not because it was impossible, but because it would kill me. I would hunt down the motherfucker who touched my wife and slice his head clean from his shoulders.

"That's what I thought."

"That's not the full picture, Avice. Ian said this went on for months, and you completely shut him out. That's a long time to be ignored by your wife. You're entitled to your grief, but abandoning your husband is unacceptable. He may have violated your marriage with his actions, but you also violated it by neglect. You assumed he prayed for this to happen, which is a horrible accusation. And I say this as respectfully as possible, bringing a child into the world at our age would be irresponsible. You romanticized it like it would be a much different experience than it really would be, not to mention the problems the child would most likely have. Your emotion has clouded your sound logic, and you let it destroy your marriage."

Her eyebrows slowly rose up her face as she tensed, and a fire sparked in her eyes the way it did with Ivory when something pissed her off. Avice kept her thoughts to herself, but her anger was visible. "Maybe all of that is true, Huntley. But the grief took over my mind, body, and heart. I had no control over it. And if you don't understand that, it's because you're lucky enough never to have experienced it yourself. Ian made a choice to fuck someone. I was *forced* to endure that depression."

It grew more challenging to carry on the conversation, because all I wanted was for the two of them to be together again. But it was complicated and messy, and talking about relationships and shit wasn't my forte. "With all due respect, Ivory and I went through the same thing, and while it was hard, she didn't shut me out. If anything, it brought us closer together."

"Because you both lost something," she snapped. "Ian didn't want it."

"You know if this had been ten or twenty years ago, his reaction would have been completely different. He never wanted Lila to be an only child, and he confided his disappointment to me on numerous occasions. I hate to say it, but you're being unreasonable about this."

"Unreasonable…"

I knew I'd taken it too far. "I just think you wouldn't have been so upset if you were more logical about the situation rather than emotional. Ian may not be your blood, but he's your family. You lost that in this crisis, but you need to get it back. Rebuild your marriage."

"He fucked someone else."

"I understand that's hard—"

"So the next time we hit a rough patch, he's going to screw someone?"

"He wouldn't, Avice."

"You never answered my question, Huntley."

A deep breath filled my lungs.

"If your mother passed away, and you were inconsolable for months—even though that would be unreasonable because she lived a long and full life—and then Ivory slept with someone else because you didn't give her the attention she wanted, would you be okay with that?"

It was difficult to picture, because if I lost my mother, I would only hold Ivory tighter rather than push her away. And no matter how bad things got between us, Ivory would never betray my trust.

"The answer is written all over your face."

"I can't give you a real answer based on a hypothetical."

She sat forward, her body leaning over the table. "If Ivory slept with another man, for any reason under the fucking sun, would you forgive her?"

I saw the world in black and white, right and wrong, lie and truth. If a woman betrayed me, we would be done. I wouldn't even give her the chance to apologize. But with Ivory, my wife, the mother of my children, the world turned gray. "I can't live without her…" I wouldn't have the self-respect to walk away. I wouldn't have the strength to move on with someone else. "I would much rather work on our marriage than let it die—because it's worth fighting for. I work hard to make my wife happy and satisfied and ensure she has no reason to ever walk away, because I would die if she ever did."

"So, this is my fault?"

"I didn't say that."

"Then you implied it."

"A tragedy struck your family, and you reacted to it. Ian reacted to your reaction. That's all I'm saying. You've been together for over twenty years and have a beautiful daughter. And I don't need to tell you how much Ian loves you—because you already know."

Now she looked away, her arms still tight over her chest.

"You both made mistakes. Let them go and save this marriage."

"I didn't make a mistake—"

"You pushed your husband away for months. That's unacceptable. Grieve all you want, but there's no reason your husband can't be a part of that. It doesn't justify what he did, but you hurt him too. While you were grieving the loss of a child that was never going to make it, he was grieving the loss of his wife."

"Don't you think you're biased—"

"I was disappointed when Ian told me what he did. I made that disappointment well-known. You're a good woman and a part of this family, and you deserve greater respect than that. But I don't think your hands are clean either. You love each other—and that's all that matters. Put this behind you and move on."

Her eyes dropped to the table.

"Avice."

"I don't look at him the same anymore."

Like my heart was the one on the line, it shattered into infinite pieces.

"I'll always picture him with that other woman."

"He hasn't been with anyone since."

"Doesn't change anything." Her eyes remained down on the table. "I needed his commitment when we were married."

"You *are* married."

"Not in my eyes."

"But you are in the eyes of the gods. Therefore, you are. Your souls are bound together, destined to be united in eternity. That's the promise you made to each other—"

"Did Ian remember that promise when he stuck his dick in someone else? Did he think about our souls being linked together for all eternity? No, all he thought about was getting his dick wet."

I'd been there for an hour and had made no progress whatsoever.

"Huntley, I appreciate what you're trying to do, but this is between Ian and me. He shouldn't have asked you to intervene in his fuckup."

"He didn't ask me."

Her eyes softened.

"This relationship is worth fighting for—and you've forgotten that."

12

HUNTLEY

Storm lowered his neck and his powerful eyes met my own.

I removed my glove so my skin could feel his scales, so the connection between us could burn like the touch of hot coals.

His eyes closed, and a quiet breath escaped his large nostrils. ***Much time has passed since I've seen your face.***

I know. I need your help.

Anything for my king. His eyes opened again, and he regarded me, his head rising.

Trouble may be stirring in our lands, threatening the peace we won decades ago.

Then I'll burn it with my fire. Break it with my teeth.

I know you will. I stood back, regarding the mighty dragon as it stood outside HeartHolme, the beauty of his scales highlighted by the torches.

How are your hatchlings?

They aren't hatchlings anymore.

Then what are they?

I struggled to find the right word so he would understand. *They're dragons now.*

Ian walked up behind me. "Ready for tomorrow?"

I turned away from Storm to face my brother. "Yes."

Ian stared at me, needing information he refused to ask for.

"I'm sorry."

His eyes immediately dulled in disappointment, the light leaving his gaze as the clouds blocked the sun. In the bar, he'd protected his emotions behind walls, but now those walls were gone.

"I'll try again—"

"It's okay."

"I know Ivory will have better luck."

"There's not enough luck in the world. Not after what I did."

My hand went to his shoulder, and I gripped the armor that he couldn't feel. He avoided my gaze, staring at the cobalt dragon before him. "We will fix this."

"If Avice were your sister and not my wife, you would hate my guts, and you know it…"

I withdrew my hand. "I don't think I would."

His eyes shifted back to mine.

"I wouldn't tell you to fight if I thought the battle was lost."

"Yes, you would—because no battle is lost to you."

"No battle is lost when we're the soldiers. We'll prevail, Ian. Like we always do."

"Thought you could sneak in and out without saying hello?"

I secured my armor in place and sat at the dining table to have breakfast like I did every morning with my family—except my wife and kids weren't present. My gaze lifted to see my sister standing there, her eyes furious just the way my wife's were whenever I provoked her.

"I had to find out from the baker, of all people." She pulled out the chair across from me and sat down. "That King Rolfe arrived in HeartHolme last night—my own brother."

Ian ate his food in silence, his head down, his sadness palpable. My mother sat at the head of the table, the seat that was rightfully mine, but I would never ask for it.

I held my sister's gaze. "It was an impromptu trip."

"So? You know where I live."

"I had a busy night—"

"Too busy for your sister?"

"Huntley was trying to help me with Avice." Ian's head remained bowed as he ate his oatmeal. It was still dusky outside, the light beginning to touch every corner of the world.

The daggers in her eyes were immediately sheathed. "Sorry, just haven't seen you in a while."

"Been busy," I said before I drank my coffee.

"Busy being bored at fancy parties?" she asked sarcastically.

I only tolerated the social bullshit because Ivory was there. She did all the talking, did all the leading. Most of the time, I zoned out completely. "I'm a father."

"Of grown-ass adults."

"You want to keep yelling at me or enjoy what little time we have?"

"Little time?" she asked. "You're leaving already?"

"Huntley and I need to make a visit to the Teeth," Ian said.

"Why?" she asked. "What's going on with them?"

I explained the situation, picking at my food because I was too tired to be hungry. I'd slept in my chambers in the castle, but it wasn't the same without Ivory beside me, using me as her mattress, her pillow, and her sheets.

"Those bastards." She shook her head. "After the mercy we granted them, they think they can fuck with us?"

"Nothing has been confirmed," I said. "We can't assume anything."

"You're taking Storm and Pyre?" she asked.

"Yes."

"Then take their armor. It might be a tight fit. They've gotten fat since they last wore it, but they'll be safer with it."

"Don't let them hear you say that." Ian spooned his oatmeal and took a bite. "They'll burn you to a crisp."

We walked out of HeartHolme to the open field where the dragons waited for us.

"How's Ivory?" Elora asked.

"Worried."

"She doesn't actually believe those morons could kill you?"

"No. But she believes her life would be over if she lost me."

"I'm not worried about it. They're powerless against the two of you and armored dragons."

"Walking into battle with arrogance is the same as walking in without a sword."

She rolled her eyes. "You always have something wiseass to say."

We stopped in front of the dragons, and that was when we noticed the tightness of the armor around their arms and bodies. It was too tight, but not tight enough to restrict their movements.

Storm lowered his gaze and looked at me. *I already have mighty scales.*

We have to be cautious.

But these scales are too tight.

You'll wear them a short while.

He released a plume of angry smoke from his nostrils.

"Doesn't like it, huh?" Elora asked.

I regarded my sister. "I'll return to Delacroix once my business has concluded. I'll see you next time."

"I barely got to see you."

"I'll return with Ivory shortly. I know she'll wish to speak with Avice herself."

She wrapped her arms around me as she rose on her tiptoes. "Well, I look forward to seeing you then. Perhaps we can get a beer and a hot stew—like old times."

I clapped her on the back before I pulled away. "I look forward to it. Give Bastian my best."

"I will."

I turned to my mother next, reading the unease in her intelligent eyes.

"Be careful, Huntley."

"Always."

"The scales of dragons and the blade of a king can't save you from deception."

I gave a nod.

"It would be unwise to provoke us after the mercy we granted, but perhaps we're the fools for granting mercy in the first place."

"We'll see you soon enough." I embraced my mother, feeling her thin frame that used to be covered with muscles. Time had ravaged the strength of her body, but it seemed like eternity was the only thing strong enough to ravage her mind. I pulled away and approached Storm.

Ian said goodbye to both of them before he mounted his dragon. "Ready?"

I nodded before Storm pushed off the ground and opened his powerful wings. With a single flap, he was hoisted high into the sky, above the city of Heart-Holme. It was a sunny day despite the bitter cold, and his scales glimmered in the light.

Pyre appeared beside me, my brother mounted in the saddle Elora had made. We both turned to the north and made our journey to the Teeth, our mighty dragons carrying us with the speed of the wind.

We dropped beneath the clouds and spotted their kingdom inserted between the mountains, snow on the peaks and the ground. The green pines were white with snow, and the world was a stark blanket of paleness.

The dragons landed on the earth with a distinct thud like an avalanche that had just halted at the bottom of the mountain. We both climbed off and hit the snow, the drifts reaching our ankles.

"Pyre, you wait here." I turned to my dragon. "Storm, circle their kingdom. Make your presence known."

Storm leaped from the ground and launched to the sky, releasing a mighty roar as he flapped his powerful wings. It rivaled the call of the yetis that occupied these very mountains. He flew directly overhead, drawing the attention of all the Teeth who lived inside.

Ian followed him with his gaze before he looked at me. "I think they know we're here."

"Damn right, they do."

We approached the enormous gate that protected their kingdom from unwanted visitors, the very gate Ivory and her brother had to climb over after she was captured. My own mother had betrayed me to hand over my wife, and before I could save her, she saved herself.

The doors began to swing forward as we approached, their machinery working hard to move something so heavy. A distinct hum from the hinges sounded in the silence, the snow absorbing the noise.

When the doors were finally open, Rancor appeared, his soldiers on either side of him, fully armed like they expected a foe rather than a friend. His skin was as white as the snow, and his dark clothing make the contrast more prominent. His teeth were secured in his jaw, looking like a man no different from Ian or me.

We approached each other, stopping on the hard earth that had been cleared of snow when the doors were cranked open.

Rancor regarded me in my full armor and glanced at Pyre, who was stationed behind me. "M'lord, it's obvious you come with open hostility, but it's not obvious why. Have we done something to offend the King of Kingdoms?" The crest on his chest bore the symbol of their people, a snake, the only other creature that could unhinge its jaw the way they could. His sword was on his hip, but he kept his hands in front of him to show his peaceful intention.

"You have provoked my hostility," I said. "And you'll provoke my wrath if you try to deceive me."

"Choose to deceive you how, m'lord?" His hands came together at his waist, his gloved fingers interlocked. "Perhaps we can discuss this inside with a feast in your honor—"

"We're not equals—and it seems you've forgotten that."

Rancor said nothing, but his angry gaze said it all.

"I've granted you the privilege to occupy these lands despite your treason. You should occupy them in silence. A rabbit doesn't invite the wolf into its den for a feast, and neither should you."

The anger simmered in his eyes, about to come to a boil. "Make your demands, m'lord."

"An unidentified black ship was spotted on the shore months ago. The corpses of two dead yetis were found halfway between here and the outpost—and my people know nothing about it. But I suspect you know exactly what I'm talking about."

Rancor was either telling the truth or had the best poker face I'd ever seen, because he looked genuinely

The Forsaken Vampire

bewildered. "We live inland, so we have no fleet of ships—"

"But someone came to pay you a visit. They landed at the coast, killed two yetis without casualties on their side, which is no easy task, and then had a meeting with you before they returned from whence they came. Does that sound right, Rancor?"

His eyes remained locked on mine, not even blinking. "We're not the friendliest, as you know. We have no distant friends or relations to invite for a glass of wine. The black ship is news to me, and it's also disturbing news that someone came to our lands without the king's permission. Should we be concerned for war?"

"You're going to look me in the eye and tell me you know nothing about this?"

"The only reason we continue to breathe is by your mercy," he said. "We're allies—not enemies. Why would we seek to oppose you?"

"Because I've taken your land and your food."

"What's the alternative?" he asked calmly. "To allow us to feed on your people? That would never work."

"I don't believe him," Ian said from beside me. "He's being far too diplomatic. If he were truly innocent, he would be annoyed and offended by the accusation."

"Who says I'm not annoyed and offended?" Rancor barked. "But I'm not stupid enough to say that to the man who could order his dragons to burn me alive with the snap of his fingers." Now Rancor did look annoyed, dropping his well-mannered politeness and showing the true monster underneath. "You have dragons, m'lord. Why didn't you follow this mysterious ship to its destination? Why are you questioning us, a race that resides in the east, far away from the coast? You're supposed to defend this continent from outside invaders, and the fact that you're questioning me, of all people, makes *me* question your fitness to lead us all."

I said nothing, but the anger spread through my system like frostbite.

"Is that what you wanted me to say?" Rancor cocked his head slightly. "As for the yetis, didn't you consider the fact that it's mating season right now? Those could have been two males fighting over one female—and killed each other."

I continued to watch his face, waiting for some sign of a lie, for a tell.

"I know you came here for answers and received insults, but that's the truth, m'lord. We may not be friends, but we're allies. We may prefer human blood to animal blood, but it's preferable to being dead. You extended us mercy despite our treason, and we'll never forget that kindness."

He played the game well, and a part of me even believed his act, but I wasn't stupid enough to show my hand. "My eye is still trained on you, Rancor. If you're innocent, you'll be granted an apology. But if you're guilty, you'll all be consumed in a ring of fire. I'll post guards outside your kingdom to monitor everyone who enters and exits these mountains. If you're innocent, you better act it."

Without a goodbye, Ian and I both turned our backs and walked to Pyre, who had his eyes trained on the Teeth behind us. Smoke issued from his nose and disappeared in the dry air above.

Storm, it's time to go.

Rooooaaaaaarrrrrr. Storm made the mountains shake before he traveled back to us, his brilliant scales appearing in the sky above us.

The Teeth were out of earshot, so Ian spoke. "What do you think?"

"I'm not convinced of his guilt or innocence."

"Neither am I."

"We'll need to keep an eye on them. But we'll need to investigate other leads as well."

"The outcasts?" he asked as he mounted Pyre.

"Yes," I said as I climbed up on Storm. "That's a start."

13

IVORY

I wore the crown in my husband's stead, the Queen and Protector of Delacroix and the Kingdoms. But it was a burden too heavy to carry alone, not when I was riddled with stress from my king's absence. I wanted to send a letter to HeartHolme to ask my mother-in-law for an update, but when it was susceptible to interception, I knew I couldn't. Until Huntley returned with news himself, I couldn't risk our enemies knowing exactly where he was and what he was doing.

So I was trapped in a prison in my mind, forced to suffer alone because my kids had no idea that danger potentially lurked across our lands. I sat at the breakfast table, Huntley's seat at the head vacant, drinking coffee because I had no appetite for food.

"Mother, are you alright?" Atticus's voice brought me back to reality, the sunlight coming through the open windows, the warmth that Huntley didn't feel down at the bottom of the cliffs.

"I think I'm coming down with a cold."

"Father's gone for a day, and you're already falling apart." The corner of his mouth lifted with the joke he made, not realizing how true his assessment was.

I forced a smile then looked into my cup of coffee, deciding to add more cream even though I didn't need it. "Your sister hasn't come down."

"She's always been lazy."

"She's usually here before you are."

"That's because I have to give orders to the soldiers at dawn before breakfast."

"I'll fetch her." I left the table and walked down the hallways until I reached her bedroom. The door was closed, so I tapped my knuckles against it several times, in the hope of gently waking her if she was asleep.

But it was quiet.

I knocked again. "Sweetheart?"

Still nothing.

I turned the doorknob and peered inside.

The bed was empty, made by the maids as if she hadn't come home the night before. I suspected she'd met someone last night and didn't fall asleep until an hour before sunrise. Perhaps she was more adventurous because her father was gone, because she knew I understood the fact that she was a grown woman exploring adult relationships, while he didn't want to think about it.

I returned to the dining table where my son ate alone.

"Where is she?"

"She's still asleep," I said. "Doesn't feel well."

"Maybe she's the one who gave you the bug."

I looked at him, eyebrows furrowed in confusion.

"Because you said you were sick?"

"Oh…that's right. That does make sense. Good thing your father isn't here to catch it."

"I don't think I've ever seen him sick."

"Neither have I."

By midday, I still hadn't seen Harlow.

She hadn't returned to her bedroom, hadn't been spotted in the castle either. I was certain she was fine, just lost track of time, found someone who made her forget all her responsibilities. But with Huntley gone, I wasn't quite myself, and I started to worry when I didn't need to worry.

When dinner arrived and she still hadn't returned, the mild concern turned into something more potent. Harlow might have lost track of time or gotten wrapped up in the throes of young love, but she would never make me wait this long to see her. She'd never pulled a stunt like this before, always sneaking back into her bedroom before breakfast so her father would never suspect a thing.

I went to General Henry, the soldier my husband had appointed decades ago, the position my son would inherit once Henry was ready to retire. "General Henry, I haven't seen Harlow since yesterday, and I'm starting to worry."

"When was the last time you saw her?"

"When we said goodbye to Huntley."

"Any idea where she could be?"

"She must be in the village. I don't know anywhere else she would go."

He gave a nod. "I'll dispatch the soldiers to look for her."

"And be discreet. I don't anyone to know that she is missing."

"Of course, Your Majesty."

"I'll speak to her friends and see if I can gather anything."

"Alright."

Before I left the castle, I ditched my dress and donned my uniform to go into town, bringing my bow and quiver of arrows, along with my blade. My heart raced in my chest with terror, and I wanted answers immediately. And if that meant I had to put a blade to someone's throat, so be it.

I went to Ethan first, afraid he'd done something to my daughter in retribution for her breaking his heart.

Ethan seemed like a nice guy, and I reminded myself of that fact, but when my daughter was missing, the stress made me think illogically.

I pounded on the door harder than I meant to, and Ethan answered it quickly, like he'd been working in the shop.

He blinked twice as he stared at me, clearly bewildered by my presence. "Uh, Queen Rolfe...Your Majesty." He opened the door wide and stepped back, giving me the space to enter his shop.

I stepped inside and ignored the statue in the center of the room as I glanced at every corner, looking for any sign of Harlow. "Ethan, I'm looking for my daughter. Have you seen her?" I faced the young man, my heart so weak it might give out, but I spoke with the confidence of someone worthy of the crown.

"You're looking for Harlow?" he asked, his eyebrows slightly raised. "I haven't seen her since last night."

"Where did you see her?"

"We talked at the bar. I tried to work things out with her...again, but she turned me down."

"Was she alone? Was she with anyone?"

He took a breath. "When was the last time you saw her?" Now he shared my unease, his fear mirroring mine exactly.

"When her father left. So, yesterday afternoon. Please answer my question."

"She was with this guy…an asshole."

"Why was he an asshole?"

He never answered the question. "I've seen her with him a couple times."

"Ethan, I need you to tell me everything you know about this guy."

His hands moved to his hips, and his gaze dropped to the floor.

"I understand you don't want to rat out Harlow, but I don't care what she does in her personal life. I just want to know she's safe. Please tell me everything you know because she's never been gone this long before, and I'm starting to worry."

He stared down for a while before he met my gaze, taking a labored breath. "His name is Aurelias. I've followed her to his cottage a couple times. I think it's been going on for about a week."

"I need you to take me to his place. Now."

"Uh, okay." He removed his apron and dropped it on the floor before he led me across the street, a short walk from the bar she frequented, and to the front door of the cottage. "This is it."

I knocked on the door. "Aurelias?" I knocked again. "Harlow?"

Ethan stood behind me and waited.

I tried the knob, and it was unlocked, so I pushed the door open to an empty house. "Harlow?" I stepped inside, seeing broken glass across the floor.

"Your Majesty, we should wait for the guards—"

"Harlow!" I stepped across the broken glass and felt it crunch under my boot. I saw a broken bottle on the floor, shining with dark blood. My heart raced with unease, and now I missed Huntley in a way I hadn't before. "Fuck." I searched the living room then went upstairs. "Harlow!" The upstairs looked untouched, the bed made, no blood anywhere.

"Your Majesty!"

I came back downstairs, seeing the cellar doors opened in the floor. "What is it, Ethan?"

"There's a body down here."

I halted at the top of the steps, my eyes already wet with tears.

"It's not Harlow."

"Oh, thank the gods…" I rushed down the steps and found Ethan crouched over a dead body. "He's been dead awhile."

I came over to see the man, pale as snow, like all the blood had been drained from his body.

"I don't recognize him."

"This isn't Aurelias?"

"No. He's young and good-looking."

My mind raced as I tried to figure out the pieces of the puzzle. "What do you know about Aurelias?"

"Nothing."

"Had you seen him around before Harlow started talking to him?"

"No. Never seen him and never heard of him."

"Huntley just left…" I turned away, talking to myself more than Ethan. "That can't be a coincidence…"

Ethan came back to me. "Your Majesty?"

I was on the verge of crying and screaming at the same time.

"What are we going to do?"

"It was all a scheme. A scheme to get Huntley to leave so Aurelias could take Harlow. That means…Huntley is in danger…and so is my daughter." The tears were about to pour down my face. I was about to curl into a ball and collapse. I was about to pray for the gods to return my husband because I couldn't do this alone. But then I swallowed all the terror and sucked in a breath so big it curbed the tears.

"What are we going to do?" he repeated.

"Prepare for war."

"I want the army divided into thirds," I told General Henry. "I want a third of our army to travel to the bottom of the cliffs to search for Harlow. Half of them will monitor the coast for ships that shouldn't be there. The other half will march to the Teeth and demand answers. We'll need to send a letter to Heart-

Holme and tell them to watch the coast on their end. I suspect Harlow's captor will try to flee by ship."

General Henry nodded. "And the other thirds?"

"One will need to stay in Delcroix in case we're attacked. The other third will scour the Kingdoms. If that asshole is hiding somewhere, we'll find him."

General Henry nodded before he placed his helmet upon his head. "I'll lead the troops to the bottom of the cliffs. Atticus will remain here to lead the others in my stead."

"Alright."

"We'll find her, Queen Rolfe."

"We better."

He walked out as Atticus rushed in.

"Someone's taken Harlow?" he asked incredulously. "And I'm just hearing about this now?"

"Son, we don't have time for this." I held up my hand to stifle his voice. "I'm leaving you in charge of Delacroix's defense while General Henry takes the others to investigate the bottom of the cliffs."

"And what about you?"

"I'll join the others as we scour the Kingdoms to the north where the port is."

"You think he's trying to take Harlow off the continent?"

"Based on the black ship your father saw, yes."

"What black ship?"

"Your father received word that a black ship had visited our shores. He went to the Teeth to investigate."

My son's face immediately hardened at the deceit. "You lied to us—"

"He tried to lie to me too. The most obvious escape route is the bottom of the cliffs because of the snow and poor visibility. But that also seems like the most obvious escape route, so I suspect this man took Harlow north, where we wouldn't pursue him."

"What does he want with my sister?"

"I don't know. But probably leverage against your father."

"Leverage for what?"

"I don't know, and I don't care."

"What about Father?"

"I just sent a letter to HeartHolme. But if he's still with the Teeth, he won't see it for a while."

His face paled. "You think he's okay?"

He'd just walked into a trap that we didn't see coming. I was afraid he was already dead. Ian too. "I'm sure he's fine. Harlow is the one we need to worry about right now."

"I should take the troops north while you stay here since you're Queen of Delacroix."

"All I care about is your sister—"

"If she's there, I'll find her. You need to be here in case HeartHolme or General Henry sends word. Or Father returns."

I didn't want to stand around and do nothing. I needed to be doing something—like stabbing my blade through that asshole's stomach for touching my daughter. But my duty was to my people as well as my family.

Atticus grabbed my shoulder and squeezed it. "Mother, it'll be alright."

"She's my daughter."

"And she's smart and strong and fearless. That guy doesn't understand who he just crossed. We'll get her back—or she'll get herself back."

The tears welled in my eyes, impossible to control. "I'm so fucking scared."

"I know." My son squeezed me again. "But we'll get her back. And if we can't, you know Father will. They didn't take her to kill her. Otherwise, they would have just slit her throat and left her behind—"

"Atticus." I didn't want that horrible image in my head.

"They took her for a reason—so we have time."

14

HARLOW

My body suddenly jolted, and I rolled onto my side. I was dead asleep, warm and tucked inside the covers, but the bump had stirred my consciousness. My last memory hit me, fighting for my life in the middle of a kitchen, and my eyes snapped wide open.

I was in the back of a wagon, and a thick tarp was pinned over the top, trapping me inside. Hooves from horses sounded against the road, and the wagon shifted left and right as we crossed rough terrain. We were at an angle, going downhill.

I tried to spring into action, but then I realized my ankles were tied together, and so were my wrists. I twisted the rope, tried to slip my hand free from the tight bindings, tried to break through the strands with brute force, but nothing worked. I would scream, but he had my mouth gagged with a rope. I crawled to the bottom of the wagon and kicked the wood, hoping the flap would come free and I'd drop on the road and be left behind. Someone else would find me and return me to Delacroix.

But then the wagon came to a halt.

Shit.

"You're smarter than you look." The flap was tugged open, and then cold air immediately rushed inside. The sky wasn't a pastel blue. It was covered with gray storm clouds as the air froze my lungs in place. His handsome face appeared, and he reached for the rope on my ankles before he dragged me back up and hooked me to the side of the wagon.

I tried to fight his hold, tried to scream past the gag, but nothing worked. There was clearly no one around anyway. Otherwise, he wouldn't have stopped. I stomped my feet against the wood of the panel and tried to break it down, but all I did was hurt my knees.

"Have at it." He lowered the tarp again and secured it closed.

I screamed through my gag, but it sounded pathetic, even to me.

"I suggest you rest while you can. It's going to get rough soon enough."

It seemed like an entire day had passed before he stopped again. The flap opened, and he looked down at me. "Look, we can play this out in one of two ways. You can appreciate my generosity by doing your business without a fuss, or I can treat you like a farm animal with no rights at all. Which do you prefer?"

I could feel the heat from my hatred radiating from my eyes as I stared.

"You'd rather hold it, then?"

I had to pee badly. And I was thirsty...and starving.

"There's nobody around, or I wouldn't have stopped. So you can scream if you want, but the only person who might come calling is a yeti, and in that case, we're both dead." He unhitched the back of the wagon. "So?"

I stared at him and gave a nod.

"Alright." He grabbed my ankles and dragged me to the edge before he undid all the knots in the binding.

Once my ankle was free, I kicked him in the face as hard as I could.

He caught my boot like he knew I was going to do it the second I was free. "You want to pee or not?" He grabbed me by the arm and placed me on my feet, my hands bound together in front of me.

I stared at him and extended my hands.

"I'll undo your pants."

I growled against the ropes over my mouth.

"The second I untie you, you're going to attack me." He moved for my pants.

I immediately stepped back and tried to force the rope out of my mouth.

He watched me struggle and took pity on me before he pulled the rope free. "What are you trying to say?"

"If you touch me, I'll kill you."

"You didn't mind me touching you before."

"Ugh, don't remind me." I extended my hands. "Untie me."

"Only if you don't cause a fuss."

"I won't."

He leaned against the wagon with his arms crossed over his chest. "I know you're lying."

"I'm not lying."

"Still lying."

"Just untie me."

"Yes, I'll get right on that."

I dropped my hands and continued to stare.

"Let me put it this way. If you fuck with me, I'll never let you use the bathroom again."

He was an opponent unlike any I'd ever faced. He was faster than my own father. He seemed to know shit he shouldn't know. Without a sword or a weapon, it seemed unlikely that I would escape in this moment. "Why are you doing this to me?"

"You want to use the bathroom or not?"

"Yes. But I also want to know why you're doing this."

He came to me and removed all the knots in the rope until my wrists came free. "You have two minutes."

I massaged my irritated skin and then stepped into the tree line. We were on the long path that my father had built into the mountain, that wound back and forth down to the bottom of the cliffs. We were almost at the bottom. I could tell by the cold. I moved behind a tree, did everything that I needed to do, and then stood there for a moment, treasuring my freedom for a couple minutes.

My two minutes were up, but he let me be.

The panic set in once I had a moment to appreciate my circumstances. I was being held as a prisoner by some mysterious man, a man I suspected wasn't a man at all. I'd hurt Ethan, someone who really cared about me, and threw myself at someone who didn't give a damn about me.

"Time's up, sweetheart."

I stayed behind the tree, not wanting to go back to my horrible reality. Had my mother realized I was missing yet? Was my father okay? Would he be able to find me once he returned? I came back from the tree line, seeing him standing there with the ropes in his hands. "Why are you doing this?"

"Does it matter?"

"Of course it matters."

He approached me and began to secure the ropes around my wrists.

I stared at him, studying his face like I'd see some glimmer of humanity in his gaze. "Where are you taking me?"

When he was finished with my wrists, he moved to my ankles and secured those before he lifted me into the wagon.

"Why are you doing this?"

He shoved the gag into my mouth and secured the rope around my head, completely heartless to all my unease.

I tried to kick him in the knee, but he sidestepped it like he knew it was coming. Then he forced me down underneath the tarp before he secured it again. "It's nothing personal, sweetheart."

I knew we reached the bottom when the incline disappeared. Now we were on flat ground. He hadn't stopped since he'd taken me, so I wasn't sure how much time had passed or if my mother had even realized I was gone.

He pulled back the flap, and instantly, the ice-cold air rushed in.

"Not so bad back here, is it?" He grabbed the knot at my ankles and dragged me close before he cut me free.

I sat up and looked at the world around us. White snow was on the ground. It covered the pine trees. I'd spent little time here because we usually traveled by dragon to HeartHolme, but my father had told me tales about his life down here in the cursed cold. When I looked at the path that wound its way back to the top, it was far in the distance.

He cut the bindings at my wrists. "Try to run if you want, but I'm faster."

"How about we race and find out?"

His eyes locked on mine before a slight smile moved on to his lips. He didn't say anything and walked to the horses. He freed them from the wagon, and one of them was secured to the saddle of the other. "You know how to ride?"

I hopped off the wagon and felt my body sink ankle-deep into the snow. It was freezing cold, and I was unprepared for it. Aurelias was in black armor with a snake on the front. The material was shiny, reflecting the light from the sky and the snow. He also wore a black cloak. It was enough to protect him in battle, but even in the extreme temperatures, he seemed unaffected by it.

He reached into the cupboard at the back of the wagon and pulled out clothing. "Put this on before you freeze." He tossed it in the back of the wagon.

I wanted to refuse out of spite, but I was too cold for that nonsense. I pulled on the waterproof boots, the fur-lined pants, and the heavy coat he must have stolen from someone else to give to me.

"Let's go."

"Let's go where?"

He walked over to the second horse, white with gray spots. "Come on. I'll help you up."

"You think I can't get on a damn horse by myself?"

"The sooner you cooperate, the sooner you'll be warm."

"And dead."

He continued to stand by the horse, giving me a cold stare. "You aren't going to die."

"Then what's going to happen to me?"

"Just get on the damn horse—"

I took off at a sprint, trying to maneuver through the uneven snow back to the inclined path. He might be faster than me, but the snow was a barrier for both of us, and if he slipped once, I would be able to take the lead.

I'd barely made it ten feet before he grabbed me and yanked me back toward the horses. "I already said you can't outrun me."

"Why are you so freakin' fast?"

He gave me another shove, forcing me back toward the horses.

"What are you?"

He ignored me and continued to drag me back to where the horses waited.

"Answer me!" I had no idea what I was up against. He wasn't human, but he wasn't one of the Teeth. He wasn't Necrosis either because I'd seen him naked countless times, and he had no spots.

He ignored me as he positioned me in front of the horse. "I don't owe you an answer."

"You tricked me into fucking you for a week—"

"I didn't trick you into doing anything you didn't want to do. You can't rewrite history because you're embarrassed. You fucked my brains out because you wanted to, sweetheart. Now, get on the damn horse."

My palm struck him across the face, moving before I could even think about the action.

He took the hit and gave a quiet sigh of annoyance.

"I should have stayed with Ethan."

He took a moment before he looked at me again. "Nice guys always finish last, don't they?" He grabbed my hips and turned me around before he lifted me and forced me to spread my legs over the saddle.

The second I had the reins, I dug my heels into the horse to take off. But the horse didn't move.

Aurelias took his time mounting the other horse, a subtle smile on his lips. "Let's go."

Aurelias rode his steed hard through the snow, heading inland away from the coast. He didn't head south toward HeartHolme, and while I'd never been there in person, I knew only one thing lived in this direction.

The Teeth.

Once the light left the sky, he directed the horses into a clearing and dismounted.

I tried to take off again, even if that meant running into the darkness, but my horse was worthless. That meant I had to mount the other horse when Aurelias wasn't looking.

Aurelias tied him to a tree, executing a series of knots like he knew exactly what I was thinking.

I dropped into the snow and immediately searched the area for old branches to make a fire.

"No fire."

"I'll freeze out here—"

"Then you'll have to get close to me." He took my horse and secured him the same way at the tree.

"Yeah, I'll pass."

"Fine by me." He grabbed a short shovel from the saddlebag and removed the snow in a small area before he dropped a bedroll on the earth, even though it was probably just as cold as the snow that had been on top of it. "Rest for a few hours. Then we'll take the horses on foot."

"In the dark?" I asked incredulously. "That's the stupidest idea I've ever heard."

"Then maybe I'll die, and you'll be free to go."

"If you die, I'll probably die too."

"Rest. I'll watch."

"So, you don't need to sleep, and you can see in the dark…"

He turned away and leaned against the nearest tree, looking into the pitch black like he could see a damn thing. His arms crossed over his chest, and he stood still, like the cold didn't bother him at all.

The shivers started immediately, and now I couldn't stop shaking.

"Zip up the bedroll completely. It'll trap your body heat inside and keep you warm."

"Sounds like you've done this before."

"Maybe I have."

"So, the Teeth pay you to kidnap people? To bring them prey to eat?"

He said nothing.

"Because I'm the worst person you could have possibly taken. When my father finds out—"

"He'll come to your rescue. Yes, that's the plan."

My heart plunged into my stomach. "This has never been about me."

He stared into the darkness.

"You want my father."

"And there's nothing he won't do for his little girl."

I launched myself out of the bedroll and rushed him, but he turned at my approach and grabbed both of my arms before I could do anything. His hands were like steel, clenching my body with the grip of a dragon's talon. He forced me back, overpowering me like my lifetime of training was inadequate.

I did the only thing I could—and screamed.

His palm immediately covered my mouth to stifle the sound, but I twisted away and screamed again. "You know what's lurking out there?"

I pushed away to scream again, but this time, he squeezed my neck and choked me out. I kicked and punched, threw my elbows hard down on his forearms like my father taught me, but this guy was made of stone.

My view quickly disappeared, and I felt myself slip away, felt my body drag as he maneuvered me to the bedroll waiting for me. I slipped under, the world turning black, and then it was over.

When I woke up, I was on the horse, tied up so I wouldn't fall off. It was dark, the moonlight barely enough to reflect off the snow around us. Aurelias guided the horse forward by the bridle, stepping into the darkness as if he could see as clear as day.

I didn't know how much time had passed. Maybe he'd packed up and left immediately once I was knocked out. Maybe he only stopped in the first place so I could rest, and once I didn't need that, he continued on.

He was in a hurry.

"How long's it been?" My voice came out like a croak. The cold didn't help either.

"A couple hours," he said. "Scream again, and I'll gag you for the remainder of this trip. Final warning."

"Fuck you."

A quiet chuckle came from the front of the horse.

"You're one of the Teeth."

"If I were, don't you think you would have noticed when you kissed me? Or when you were pushing your pussy into my face?"

"Wow…fuck you."

He didn't issue a chuckle this time. Didn't seem to care at all.

"Untie me."

He brought the horse to a stop before he walked over and untied my bindings, his face still handsome despite the rough elements, despite the fact that he hadn't slept in who knew how long. He was perfectly preserved, his face always chiseled, his eyes bright like he'd just woken up.

I rubbed my wrists when my hands were free, and he started to pull the horse again. Now that the danger had passed, the cold sank into my flesh and bones, and I winced as the wind struck my skin. A powerful gust swept through, and snow hit me right in the face. "If you aren't one of the Teeth, why are you taking me to them?"

"For a princess, you have a good sense of direction."

I hated the way he said *princess*, like it was synonymous with damsel in distress. "I'm more than a princess. I'm the future Queen of Delacroix, Heart-Holme, and all the Kingdoms across this continent—and I know exactly where you're taking me."

He ignored me.

"Answer my question."

"Sorry, sweetheart, but you aren't my princess. I don't owe you anything."

"You have to be a really heartless piece of shit to do what you did and escort me to my death."

"And you would be right."

Powerless, I sat on that horse and tried to think, tried to think about what my father would do. "If I'm going to die, you may as well tell me who you are."

"I already said you aren't going to die. Just keep your mouth shut, and they'll let you go."

"Well, I never keep my mouth shut, and I'm not letting anything happen to my father."

"That's your prerogative."

"Just tell me."

There was a long pause before he answered. "You wouldn't believe me if I told you."

I thought of the black ship Uncle Ian had spotted on the coast, a ship no one could identify. "You aren't from this land. You're from somewhere else…somewhere far away."

He remained quiet.

"Why travel all the way here to do the bidding of monsters?"

"Because I needed something from those monsters."

"I'm sure I could meet their price—and double it."

He brought the horse to a standstill.

My heart raced with a surge of hope.

He moved to where I sat on the horse, looking up at me with his gloved hands still secure on the reins. "They've already completed their end of the deal. I'm bound by my honor to fulfill my promise."

"Honor? If you had any honor, you would be saving me."

He looked away, seeing the path in the darkness that I couldn't make out. "As I said, it's nothing personal." He started to pull the horse again, directly into the wind and the snow.

Dawn came, and the snowy mountains were visible on the clear day. Without the cloud coverage, it was even colder, so cold that I actually looked forward to my captivity with the Teeth just so I would be warm.

My father had told me he would visit the Teeth for a conversation. Perhaps I would get lucky and arrive when he was already there. Just as the thought passed through my mind, my eyes lifted to the two colored dots in the sky. At first, I thought they were birds, but as they drew closer, I saw the brilliance of their scales.

I quickly glanced at Aurelias. His eyes seemed to be on the mountains ahead, oblivious to the skies.

When they came closer, I opened my mouth and screamed as loud as I could. "Father!" I waved my arms frantically, hoping the dragons would hear my cry, that they would look down and see me throwing my arms about to get their attention. "Father!"

Aurelias tugged me off the horse and threw me in the snow. He secured his hand over my mouth, and he gagged me before he tightened the ropes around my head.

My eyes went up, seeing the scales pass across the sky and disappear.

15

AURELIAS

Her father passed by with two enormous dragons—and I could have lost my head. But he was too high to hear her screams, too set on his destination to notice the two figures below. I could defeat her father in battle, but I couldn't defeat him when he had a dragon.

I kept her gagged the rest of the way. She'd already given me a headache with all the questions, with all the attempts to run away and knee me in the groin. The sooner I delivered her to the Teeth, the sooner I could return home where I belonged. My father must have been angry when Kingsnake returned and I didn't. He must also be angry that I still hadn't returned, even though months had passed.

Maybe they assumed I was dead.

We approached the gate to the Crags, the Teeth's kingdom, and once they recognized me in the distance, the guards opened the gate to allow me entry.

Harlow started to fight the bindings on the horse, doing whatever she could in a desperate attempt to free herself. But the rope was too tight, and she didn't have the brute strength to tear through thick strands like that.

Once we entered the kingdom and the gate shut behind me, she stopped trying.

I pulled her down from the horse and cut the bindings around her ankles so she could walk.

She kept a straight face, looked indifferent, but inside, she was swamped by a tidal wave of fear. I could feel it in the chasm of her chest, feel the racing of her heart, the desperation inside her small little body.

I lowered my voice and addressed her. "Just do what they say, and they'll let you go."

Her eyes shifted to me, and the hatred in that gaze was so potent it was nearly poisonous. If her hands were free, they would be around my neck that very moment, squeezing the life out of me. She jerked her head back—and spat on me. "My father will flay you alive—and then feed your skin to his dragon."

I let the spit sit on my face. Didn't feel like an insult when I'd felt that same spit in my mouth and on my dick. My eyes shifted away and looked at Rancor as he approached, dressed in all black, a subtle grin on his face. "Took longer than expected, but you've paid your debt." His eyes were on Harlow, looking her up and down carefully. "She has her father's eyes."

She spat on him just the way she'd spat on me.

Rancor slowly wiped it away with his cloak. "And his spirit." He snapped his fingers. "Take her away."

Two Teeth moved in on her, and she swung her arms at one and hit him in the face with both fists. Then she kicked the other right in the knee. It all happened quickly, like she'd been waiting for the right moment. And then she took off, picking a random direction and sticking to it.

I didn't chase after her. My job was done.

Rancor nodded to the others, and then an entire fleet was after her. "We'll have fun playing with her."

My eyes shifted back to his, feeling a darkness pool in my stomach at his words. "You know what they say. You aren't supposed to play with your food."

A grotesque smile moved on to his face, showing extra teeth I didn't possess. "Yes. But food is rarely as succulent and beautiful."

The tightness was still in my stomach, a flood of unease I hadn't felt since the dragons passed by. "I doubt you'll make much progress with King Rolfe once he knows what you've done with his daughter."

"It won't matter. She'll be dead before he gets here anyway."

The numbness kicked in, the kind that made me lose sensation in both my feet and hands. The cold didn't affect me at all. I could have been next to a warm fireplace and wouldn't know the difference. "That wasn't the plan."

"Well, plans changed. King Rolfe was just here before you arrived."

"I saw the dragons overhead. What happened?"

"He spotted your ship. Accused me of doing exactly what I'm doing—betraying him. It's been a long time since I've spoken to him. I'd forgotten about his intelligence and paranoia."

"It's not paranoia if it's true."

He gave a shrug. "It matters not now. He's powerless to change what's been done."

"If you kill her, you'll have no proof."

"I can send her clothes, a lock of hair, all sorts of proof. Make her write a letter and kill her... The possibilities are endless."

The numbness turned to sickness. When I betrayed a man who didn't have my loyalty, I felt no guilt because he was a stranger. Kings died, and new ones were crowned every day. Her father knew the risks when he took on the role of sovereign. But his daughter...that was a different story. "You said you would only use her as leverage. You said nothing of killing her."

He eyed me, that smile still there. "Is that affection I detect?"

"I'm only repeating the terms of the deal—which you changed."

"And like I said, King Rolfe's visit changed everything."

"You don't have to kill her—"

"I'll kill her. And then when he shows up, I'll kill him. Then the only one standing in my way is his queen—and I'll force myself between her legs before I slit her throat."

I felt affection for no one except my father and brothers, so I didn't care about Harlow and the members of her family, but I was disturbed, nonetheless. To be responsible for the bloodshed about to ensue left a bad taste in my mouth. "All I needed was snake venom, making this a very uneven trade."

"Then what else do you want, Aurelias? A bite before you go?"

I hadn't craved her blood, not once. Everything had been set in motion, and now there was nothing I could do to stop it. Even if I returned to Delacroix to tell her father the truth, she would be dead long before I even got there. What was done could never be undone now. "Tell me where my ship is, and I'll be on my way."

His smile disappeared, and he shifted his gaze away. "King Rolfe and Steward Rolfe are watching the coast from the north to the south. There's no way I can get you on a ship without exposing my neck."

"But you're about to expose your neck anyway."

"The coast is being watched. My connections won't be able to fulfill my requests."

I stepped forward, my anger getting the best of me. "We made a deal, Rancor. I bring you the princess, and you get me home on a ship."

"It'll have to wait."

"*To wait?*" I asked incredulously. "Even if King Rolfe hands himself over, you still have to defeat all the Kingdoms. This was a suicide mission to begin with, and I'm not going to wait around in the hope you'll prevail so I can get home. Now, get me a damn ship."

Rancor stepped back, his hands moving to his sides, one hand close to the hilt of his sword. "I'm sure you could travel to the port city and pay for a ship. I can give you gold to pay off the sailors in your employ."

I had to control my voice. Had to control my hand before I did something violent. "I risk my life to bring you this girl, and you desert me?"

"It was never my intention to desert you, Aurelias. It's unfortunate that King Rolfe has grown suspicious of us. That was an outcome I didn't anticipate. And you can't blame me for that because it was *your* ship that he spotted. It was *your* negligence that compromised my plan. You're welcome to our hospitality until you're ready to leave, but you'll need to find your own arrangements for traveling back home."

16

HARLOW

"Don't touch me!" I tried to run away, but the room was small and I had nowhere to go. When one came at me, I slammed down with both of my hands in the binding and knocked him out. Two of them converged on me at once, and then I was flipped onto my back and dragged by my ankles.

I tried to grab on to anything I could to pull myself free, but it was just roots from weeds and plants. When I found a rock, I threw it at one of the Teeth, but all it did was make him kick me.

I was dragged into a prison cell in one of the buildings, a room with bars over the windows and a mattress in the corner. They dropped my feet, but before I could get up, they grabbed my boots and tugged them off.

"What the fuck are you doing?" I pushed away, feeling them grab my pants and start to tug them down. "I'll fucking kill you!" Another Teeth joined the attack, holding me down so they could pull off my clothes. My pants came down and then they took my underwear. "No!" My anger was so potent it erupted as tears, refusing to let this horrible thing happen to me.

They took my sweater and my top, taking my bra too, leaving me completely naked.

But then they stopped.

My wrists were bound to a steel chain against the wall, and they tossed my clothes on the other side of the room, far out of my reach. I squatted down with my knees to my chest, covering my body the best I could.

The silence was deafening, and I sat there with hot tears burning my eyelids. I wanted to break down and cry, but my mother would never do that, and my father certainly wouldn't. A future queen shouldn't give in to the fear, no matter how bleak the future seemed. I closed my eyes for a bit, forced myself to calm down, forced myself to think about the next step.

When I opened my eyes again, all I saw was an empty room with bars over the window. The door might or might not be locked, but I was on a short leash, so I couldn't exactly walk out of there. I needed something strong enough to break this chain free, but all I had was a mattress on the floor.

That meant I had to wait for someone to come for me —and kill them.

I rested my head against the wall and pictured the blue sky above me, the two dragons soaring overhead. "Why didn't you hear me?"

Hours passed, and I was left to sit there alone, afraid of what would become of me. My father might save me— or we might both die. If only Pyre and Storm could return, they would be able to burn all these monsters alive and carry me to safety.

Then the door opened.

I flinched at the sound, my guard up and ready to execute my plan. If I could kill them, they might have a weapon I could use to cut myself free.

The door shut again, and I looked to see my attacker, hoping it wasn't the man I'd spat on.

But it was Aurelias.

I tightened my body further, even though he'd already seen me buck naked plenty of times.

He stared at me for a moment, and as if he realized he shouldn't, he quickly averted his gaze and walked to where my clothes lay in the corner. He gathered them up and returned them to me, setting them beside me.

I stared at them, unable to put them on because of the way my wrists were bound.

He moved for my underwear, like he was going to help me step inside them.

"You want to help me? Cut me free." He was the one who'd put me in there, so that wasn't likely to happen.

He stared at the steel secured around my wrists, as if contemplating it.

"What are you doing?"

"I'll get you out of here." He lowered his chin and looked at me again. "But you need to do something for me."

A smartass comment came to mind, but it never came out of my mouth because survival was all that mattered. I would give anything to get out of there, even my right hand. "Name it."

"I want a galleon with a crew to take me wherever I wish."

I didn't ask any questions. "Fine."

"We have a deal?" He looked me in the eye, searching for a trace of a lie.

"A ship is a small price to get out of here. Now cut me free."

He pulled out a dagger, the blade black like the rocks near the sea, and started to pick at the metal, trying to mimic a key that would open the lock. He kept at it for minutes, his blade slipping and scratching the surface of the metal.

"You don't have a key?"

"If I did, you think I'd waste my time with this?"

"You're stupid enough to hand me over to the Teeth and then free me, so—"

"I'll be able to concentrate a lot better if you shut up."

I turned quiet, letting him work the lock over and over, scraping metal against metal. But then a lock finally clicked—and one hand was free. "Oh, thank the gods." I pulled my hand tight to my body, covering my chest with my arms instead of my knees.

He did the same with the other lock, finally snapping it free. "Get dressed."

"Did you think I was going to take a nap?"

"Shut. Up."

"You. Shut. Up." I quickly pulled on all my clothes, getting dressed as quickly as possible, even though Aurelias was kind enough to turn around and look the other way. I hadn't had my sword, so I had everything I came with. "How are we going to get out of here? The gate is too high."

"We're going to climb."

"You don't think they'll see us climb up the gate?" I asked skeptically.

"We're climbing the mountains."

"Did you just say mountains?"

"Yes." He turned to look at me. "It's the only way I can get you out of here. Can you do this or not?"

"I can do it, but—"

"There is no but. Yes or no."

"Yes."

"Then follow me." He poked his head out the door first, and once the coast was clear, he motioned me to follow him.

We snuck to the edge of the city, in one of the districts that seemed to be deserted and right up against the rocky outcropping. It was dark, so the juts and indentations in the mountains were hard to see. I'd never climbed a mountain before, let alone in the dark.

"Go."

"Me?" I asked in disbelief. "I don't know what I'm doing—"

"I can't catch you if I'm above you."

"Who said I needed you to catch me?"

"Do you ever stop talking?"

"Nope. Never."

He took a deep breath, like a moment of air was necessary to tolerate me. "Just. Go."

I grabbed on to the rock, found a crack for my fingers, and then hoisted myself up.

"Don't look down. Move as quickly as possible."

I rolled my eyes and kept going, finding grooves for my fingertips before hoisting myself up. My boots hung on some ledges and helped me climb. When there was nothing above me, I had to shift sideways, which took me longer to get to the top. Whenever I did look beneath me, Aurelias was right there, watching me as if he expected me to fall.

"I told you not to look down."

"Just checking on you—"

"Don't worry about me."

I tried to reach my next hold, but it was too far away, and I couldn't stretch my fingers all the way. Then his big hand moved to my ass and gave me a lift. I was able to grab it, and then his hand left my behind.

I'd rather him not help me, but I'd also rather get away.

We continued to climb, the sunlight shining right on us on the mountain.

"How has no one spotted us?"

"Because they prefer darkness over sunlight."

"But still…"

"Keep moving."

I kept going, finally reaching a plateau where I could rest. I pulled myself over the edge then lay there, catching my breath, not realizing how tired I was until I was finally allowed to stop.

Aurelias pulled himself over a moment later, but he wasn't out of breath like I was. "We'll climb until we reach snow. Then we can't go any farther without losing our grip on the rock." He moved against the rock face, standing in the shade as he looked down at the kingdom of the Teeth. "Let's go."

"Just give me a sec—"

"We don't have a second."

"They can't see us—"

"Are you the same woman who can hold her own against the King of Kingdoms?" He stepped forward and looked down at me as if he despised me. "Because it doesn't seem like it." He turned to the rock, ready to keep going whether I joined him or not.

I felt the rage burn everything, including my fingertips. I could face my father on the battlefield, but I had no experience rock-climbing. The two activities weren't comparable. I pushed myself up and came to his side, looking at the first groove for my fingers. I released a sigh of annoyance before I mapped out my initial movements. Then I grabbed the hold and pulled myself up.

"Attagirl."

I stopped everything I was doing to look at him.

He met my gaze, his eyes cold despite the encouragement he'd just given me. "What?"

I looked at the mountain again and grabbed the next hold. "Nothing."

Once we reached the snow, we stopped climbing upward and moved west, heading back to the coast on unexplored terrain. It was harder to navigate up here because we were at a constant incline. And the snow wasn't thick over the rocks, so it was easy to slip.

Not to mention, it was cold as fuck.

I gritted my teeth and didn't complain, because I would rather be cold fully dressed than naked and a prisoner of the Teeth. The sun had set, and now only a few rays of light shone over the horizon. It was already infinitely colder.

Aurelias continued to march on, like the lack of daylight was no obstacle in his determination.

I halted. "You can't be serious right now."

He looked toward the west, one foot planted on a rock as he gazed over the land. He stared for a few seconds before he turned and looked at me again, his spine still straight despite the weight of his armor and weapons.

"We're going to break our legs if we continue."

His hard expression was empty, his thoughts bottled deep inside.

"They aren't going to find us up here. They don't have dragons."

"If we stop moving, you may freeze to death."

"Me? What about you?"

"The cold doesn't bother me."

"Bullshit, it doesn't bother you. You'd have to be a yeti for it not to bother you."

He continued his stare, his hand moving to the hilt of his sword to rest. "We don't have a sleeping bag to keep you warm through the night. I fear you'll get sick and die from complications."

"I don't get sick."

A smug grin moved his lips. "Because you're royalty."

My eyes narrowed. "I work my ass off for my kingdom."

"Yes, fucking sculptors and sharing pints of ale with your friends in the bar looks like tough work."

"Fuck you, Aurelias. Every member of my family dedicates their life to Delacroix. My brother serves in the army, my father trains like we're always on the brink of war, and my mother takes care of our people. I'm prepared to take the crown when my time comes and smite my enemies."

"Still not the same thing as backbreaking work in the fields every day, *Your Highness*."

"You're a hypocrite."

"Am I?"

"I don't know *who* or *what* you are, but I know you're important. I'm sure you have a very comfortable life."

As our conversation wore on, the remaining sunlight faded from the sky. Now it was just shadows and darkness. His eyes shifted away, and he looked elsewhere, his handsome face hardened in thought.

"If you want to stumble in the dark, go for it. But I'm staying put." I moved to a nearby rock, wiped off the snow, and then sat on the cold-ass stone. I brought my knees to my chest to keep the warmth close, but I still felt icicles every time I breathed.

Instead of arguing with me, he walked off and disappeared.

Did he really just leave me?

I refused to call for him, refused to admit I would probably die out here alone.

He returned moments later, carrying a stack of branches. He made a pile on top of some rocks and then lit a match. It took a while for the flames to grow and spread, but they eventually licked the wood and made a bonfire.

"I thought you said no fires." I moved close to the flames and squatted down, feeling the warmth melt all the ice off my face.

He stood on the other side of the flames, looking into the dark forest behind us. "We have no other choice—because you'll die without it." He unclasped the cloak from his armor then walked over to me, wrapping the material around my body and placing the hood over my head.

"What about you?" I took it without complaint, knowing if I didn't get warm, a sickness would enter my lungs.

He walked back to the other side of the fire. "I told you the cold doesn't bother me."

"Well, you aren't covered in fur, so how is that possible?"

He looked into the forest again, like he could actually see something besides darkness. "You should get some sleep."

"What about you? You don't need sleep either?"

His eyes darted to me, his gaze cold. "Not as much as other people do."

"Seriously...*what* are you?"

He stared at the forest, one boot propped on a rock with his hand on the hilt of his sword.

"You're just not going to tell me?"

"I have no obligation to you. I apologize if that was unclear."

"No obligation to me? Sounds like you've said that line before."

He still didn't look at me. "Sleep. I'll stay on watch."

"You haven't slept in two days—"

"I appreciate your concern, but it's misplaced."

My eyes moved to the fire in front of me, treasuring the searing heat that filled the inside of the cloak and warmed my body. The stone beneath my ass was still cold, but soon, the fire would heat that too. I didn't want a confrontation with a yeti, but I was so cold that I was willing to take the risk. "Why did you save me?"

"I told you I needed a ship."

"You didn't need one before?"

"Rancor promised me voyage as part of the deal. He lied."

"But you took me. So you didn't complete your end of the deal either."

He turned to look at me. "I delivered you into their hands as promised. The task was completed. Now, my needs have changed, so our interests are no longer aligned. I owe them nothing."

"So, if you didn't need a ship, you would have left me there to die?"

He looked away.

"They wouldn't have stripped me naked and tied me up like that if they intended to let me go—and we both know it."

He remained focused on our surroundings despite the intensity of our conversation.

"So, if I couldn't get you a ship, I would have been raped, tortured, and killed…" Heartless wasn't the right word to describe him. He was barbaric, leaving me to a horrible fate without a burden on his conscience.

"Just be grateful that our interests are aligned."

17

HUNTLEY

Delacroix was in sight from the sky, and I could already feel the heat before we landed. My knuckles thawed in their gloves, my skin felt less dry as the humidity struck my body. The windows of the castle reflected the sunlight in a prominent glare, making it look like it was on fire.

I flew to the clearing and landed Storm, Ian landing Pyre beside me. I dropped to the ground, gave Storm a pat on the snout, and then headed toward the gate of the castle, knowing my wife would be running down the hill from the castle any second now.

Ian came to my side, and silently, we moved past the guards at the gate.

That was when I spotted Ivory appear at the top, running at full speed down the path toward me.

I grinned when I saw her, running right to me, dressed in her uniform like the queen that she was. A part of me felt bad that Ian had to witness something that he'd lost, but I was too happy about seeing her to care.

But when she drew closer, I realized this wasn't a happy moment.

Her face…it was contorted in a way I'd never seen before.

It made me stop in my tracks.

She made it to me, but instead of jumping into my arms and crushing her mouth against mine, she nearly broke down in sobs. "Someone took Harlow!" Out of breath because she had sprinted all the way from the castle to tell me, she gripped her side like there was a stitch in it.

A few seconds passed as my thoughts remained blank, my mind protecting me from the horror I couldn't face. But the mercy was short-lived, and the ugly truth hit me like a sledgehammer right against my chest.

I digested that news as a victim, not as a king who would burn the world to the ground in the name of treason. I stared at my wife as my body became immobile, the agony so unspeakable.

Ian stood beside us and said nothing, equally horrified.

The only reason I snapped out of it was because of the tears in my wife's eyes, the way she was barely holding on, sick from the toxicity of this information. She was too weak to handle this, too broken to be the fierce soldier she was.

So I had to. "Tell me everything."

"Two days ago." She sobbed through it all. "I suspected Ethan, but then he told me about this other man she was seeing…and took me to the cottage where he'd spotted them together. There was a dead body in the basement…" She paused to sob again. "I think he took her…"

It was like a knife being stabbed in my eye over and over again, and I had to stare at the blade point-blank. "What's his name?"

"Aurelias."

"What does he look like?"

"I—I don't know," she said. "General Henry took a portion of our army down to the bottom of the cliffs to search for her. Atticus took his own brigade north to the Kingdoms to search. I stayed behind... only because I had to." She continued to gasp for breath, to breathe through the tears that wouldn't stop.

I turned to look at Ian.

His face was pale as he stared back.

"This is no coincidence."

He shook his head. "I just had the same thought."

Ivory shifted her gaze back and forth between us. "What did you discover about the Teeth?"

I looked at my wife again. "They pled innocence and naivety, and I stupidly believed them." Harlow may have been there at the same time...and I'd left her there. "I'll get her back, Ivory."

The sobs stopped, but the tears glistened like raindrops on her cheeks. "I—I can't go on if you don't."

"I know." I grabbed both sides of her face and kissed her forehead before I abruptly turned away and returned to our dragons.

"Huntley?"

Ian was in the process of climbing up onto Pyre. We'd already had a long journey, but now our bodies were invigorated with rage. I turned back to Ivory as I stood in front of Storm.

She shook as she stood there, like the rage inside her was a wildfire. "Burn them all."

The dragons had covered half the continent in a single day, but they flew twice as hard even though their stomachs were empty and their energy reserves were depleted. And they roared across the sky—like they wanted the Teeth to know we were coming.

Atop my dragon and alone in the sky, I didn't have to harden my expression and turn my heart to stone. Rage electrified my nerves like lightning in a storm, and my body felt stronger than it ever had, even stronger than it'd been decades ago when I'd defeated the Three Kings with my blade.

But I was scared. More scared than I'd ever been in my fucking life.

If I lost my wife, I would be inconsolable. But to lose my daughter...to picture what they were doing to her...was enough to make me end my own life just to make the suffering stop. I'd fought for freedom, and I'd fought for love—but I'd never fought for something so important.

We'll save your hatchling, Huntley.

I said nothing, felt nothing as the ice-cold air struck me in the face.

They will release her when they see our fire, claws, and teeth.

It was dark now, because we'd spent the daylight flying from HeartHolme to Delacroix. It was dangerous to approach with limited visibility, but there was no danger strong enough to deter me.

A lifetime later, the dragons lowered closer to the ground to search for the Teeth kingdom, the Crags, and after several turns, they located it in the mountains. Storm released a stream of fire that illuminated the buildings alone.

Pyre released his fire and burned all the trees that surrounded their kingdom, bringing the dark city into the light. They had no torches and no lights on in any of the windows, as if they'd hoped we wouldn't be able to find them in the complete darkness.

Storm burned the other trees, making a ring of fire in the mountains that displayed the city with a brightness that rivaled sunlight. Teeth didn't run around the ground or leave the buildings. No one was on guard on the wall.

Take me down.

Storm landed on the earth, making the ground tremble under his weight.

I slid off and pulled my sword out of my scabbard simultaneously, ready to strike down the Teeth that rushed me.

But nobody came.

The kingdom was abandoned.

Ian continued to fly above, to provide aerial protection as I walked through the buildings and approached the gate. The wall should be manned with guards and archers, but I found no one. I took a torch off the wall, lit it with Storm's snout, and then searched the kingdom alone, opening unlocked doors, looking for evidence anyone had been there at all.

When it was clear it was abandoned, Ian landed and slid off Pyre. "No one's here."

I stood and surveyed the reflection of the fire on the buildings, searching for a sign of life.

"Could they be hiding in the mountains?"

I'd come here to save my daughter—but I knew she was gone. "They left the second we turned our backs."

"Because they knew…"

They knew I would discover the truth the second I returned to Delacroix.

"But where could they have gone? There's nowhere to hide that many people in our lands." Ian walked beside me, armed with his sword with no one to fight.

"East."

Ian finished surveying a building before he looked at me. "There's no way to cross the mountains except by flight."

"They didn't go over the mountains—they went *under* them."

Ian's cheeks paled to the color of snow. "If that were true, that tunnel would have to be hundreds of miles long."

"Yes. And it would take decades to complete..." As I said the words, I knew they were true. That from the moment we'd won the war, they'd been planning this revenge.

"Why take Harlow if they're just going to flee our lands?"

My mind worked furiously, knowing that my daughter's life was at stake. "They must have taken her as leverage against me."

"Yes, but why?" he snapped. "What does he want from you?"

"To surrender our lands to the Teeth. And if I refuse... he has allies to help him."

"What allies?"

"Whoever lurks in the east," I said. "Like I said, this plan has been in motion for a very long time...the moment Harlow was born…the moment I became vulnerable."

Ian stared, the cold winter breeze blowing his hair back. "Let's fly there in the morning."

"They're making the journey on foot, so it'll take a very long time for them to complete that journey in a tunnel."

"Then we prepare for battle with the dragons."

"They'll anticipate that, so there must be a reason they're unafraid of that outcome."

"Huntley, we need to save Harlow—"

"*You think I don't know that?*" I snapped, nostrils flaring. "You think I'm not dying inside this very fucking moment? But I'm responsible for more than just my children, but my wife, my people, and our dragons. If we execute this, it must be done right, because my daughter's life depends on it. Rushing into it blindly is exactly what Rancor and his allies want. If they capture me, the Kingdoms will fall. Ivory will be unable to lead if she loses us both. Atticus will think irrationally as well. I'm the only one capable of doing this—so it must be done right." The tears burned my eyes when I didn't know they'd formed. Now my face was hot, my eyelids burning like pepper seeds had been rubbed into the creases. I'd taken back the Kingdom that was stolen from my father, and now the past had repeated itself. But I'd lost something I couldn't afford to lose—my daughter.

Ian watched me, and once the emotion in my face became too much to withstand, he averted his gaze.

I stood there, surrounded by fire and isolation, having no plan to rescue one of the people I loved most. I felt worthless for the first time in my life, completely inadequate, feeling like I'd failed my family and my people.

Ian came to me, his hand moving to my shoulder, and the sheen in my eyes was now in his. "They didn't take Harlow to kill her—so that means we have time. We'll find her, Huntley. And she's strong enough to endure until we arrive."

I breathed harder, doing my best to fight the weakness I would never show in front of my wife, in front of anyone except my brother. I blinked several times, but it wasn't enough to stop the moisture that flooded my eyes and streaked down my cheeks.

"We'll find her," he repeated, his eyes mirroring mine. "We will."

18

AURELIAS

We traveled through the mountains, heading west toward the sea, and I had no idea what to expect as we came closer. I hardly knew this world, and the map Rancor had given me wouldn't help with this trek through the mountains. We would have to make our way down at some point, but with so much snow, that would be a dangerous descent.

Despite the inhospitable conditions, Harlow kept up with me, but I suspected pride was her primary motivation. It was the first time her emotions were nonexistent, like she was numb down to the bone, so accustomed to the cold, the famine, the misery.

I was hungry, had been hungry for a few days now, but I couldn't risk her knowing the truth about me. The less she knew, the better.

"I need to rest."

I turned around to see her sit on a rock, still wearing my cloak for warmth, utterly exhausted. "I'm surprised you lasted as long as you did."

"I'm stronger than I look."

"Your story matches the cover."

She turned her head slightly to look at me. "What's that supposed to mean?"

"What you see is what you get."

"Again, what does that mean?"

We still had a few hours of daylight, and now that the wind had stopped, the world was clear. It was white as far as the eye could see, so quiet it was eerie. There were no signs of life around us, but I wasn't fooled into a false sense of security.

"I'm starving. We need to hunt."

"What do you want?"

"I'm sorry, is this a restaurant with a menu?" she asked like a smartass.

I walked off and abandoned the conversation, her attitude hostile even when she was subdued. "Stay here. Don't move."

"Whatever."

I unsheathed my blade and set it beside her.

She eyed it before she looked at me. "What are you doing?"

"In case you need it." I walked off, heading into the woods with my bow in my hands. I moved into the distance, close enough to hear her if she called for help, and then I squatted down in the bushes and waited. It took thirty minutes, but finally, a rabbit hopped across the ground to get some sun, and I killed it with one shot. My brothers and I used to hunt when we were human. We were responsible for putting dinner on the table. Whenever we failed, we went to bed hungry, a lesson my father wanted to teach. As men, we were responsible for providing for our families, and failure had real consequences.

I returned, and when she saw the rabbit in my hand, she said, "I can clean and dress it since you hunted."

"Just make a fire—a small one."

My sword was against the rock where I'd left it, and she got to work making a small fire with a makeshift spit made out of dead branches. We got the meat on, and after cooking it to remove the pink from the flesh, I told her to eat.

"What about you?"

"I don't need it." There wasn't much meat to eat, and since I didn't eat anyway, I didn't want to waste it to keep up appearances.

"You haven't eaten in just as long as me—"

"I'll hunt if I'm hungry. Eat so we can get moving."

She dropped her argument and ate the entire thing with her fingers, cleaning off by rubbing snow across her lips and palms. "I can see the ocean. We're getting close. But how are we going to get down?"

"I have no idea."

"We can't climb."

"We'll have to find a way once we get closer."

"Or we can go back the way we came—"

"Suicide."

"And you think climbing down a snowy mountain isn't?" she snapped.

"Look, I could have just left you there and rode off on a horse. I'm only stuck up here because I saved your life—"

"Because you needed me for a ship, asshole."

I released an irritated sigh, feeling a subtle migraine behind my temple because I was hungry and tired. Getting the venom from the golden serpents had come at great sacrifice—and I'd better be rewarded for it when I returned home. "Let's keep moving. We need to cover as much ground as possible before dark."

We had a clear view of the ocean just before dark, and I knew we didn't have much farther to go. The mountains jutted up against the cliff, and the only way higher was the path carved into the rock.

That meant we had to go down.

She got to work starting the fire for the night.

We'd gotten lucky these last few nights, with no one on the mountains spotting our small campfire and the smoke that wafted up into the sky, and I feared our luck would soon run out. But if she didn't stay warm, she would probably die. I could tell she was sick by the way her voice sounded different. She did her best to hide it, like being sick was a sign of weakness, and I feared it would turn into something more serious if I didn't get her back quickly.

She sat in front of the fire, the cloak tight around her, and she said nothing as she stared at the flames. Even when she was sick and cold and in the same clothes for several days in a row, she was still a beautiful woman. The elements could conquer a mountain, but they couldn't conquer her looks.

"You need to get some sleep."

"What about you? You don't sleep, eat, or wear a cloak, and you're fine..."

Now I knew she was intimidated by me, that she felt pressured to keep up or she would look weak in comparison. It was a competition, but if she knew what I really was, she would know it was a competition she couldn't win. "You don't have to prove anything to me, Harlow."

"I'm not proving anything."

"Then sleep."

"How can I sleep on a cold rock in the snow?" she asked incredulously. "I've tried, and it doesn't work."

"If you don't sleep, your cold will turn into pneumonia and kill you."

"I'm not sick—"

"You said you weren't trying to prove anything."

Her arms circled her knees, and she pulled them close, her eyes glaring into mine before going back to the fire. "I dropped my guard around you, and you made a fool out of me. I won't do that again."

"And pretending you aren't sick and cold and tired does that, how?"

"My father always said to never let your enemies know your weakness." Her eyes moved back to mine, and there was a surge of anger that accompanied it, anger so powerful I could feel it despite her waning strength.

"When I said it wasn't personal, I meant it—"

"Yes, it definitely wasn't personal... That's for sure." Her eyes looked at the fire again. "I should have known."

"There's no way you could have known."

"Why would a man like you be interested in a woman like me..."

Harlow spoke her mind unapologetically, so I always knew how she felt, but I couldn't decipher the meaning of her words. "What does that mean?"

"Seriously?" She looked at me again. "You're really going to make me say it?"

"I genuinely don't understand."

She rolled her eyes. "*Look at you.*" She gestured with her hand, moving from my head to my toes. "You're too good to be true, and I should have assumed you only wanted something from me. That's a mistake I'll never repeat."

I still didn't understand, because she was a beautiful woman who could have any man she wanted. "I still would have wanted you if the circumstances were different."

Her eyes were focused on the fire, as if she'd tuned me out.

"You need to sleep. Your body can't fight your cold if you're exhausted."

"I don't need you to worry about me, alright?"

"Well, if you die, then I don't get my ship."

"How many times do I have to say it?" Her eyes went back to mine. "It's too fucking cold."

"Then I'll lie with you. It'll keep you warm enough to sleep—"

"I'd rather die out here in the cold than let you touch me." She had been calm a second ago, but now her words were sharp like the tip of a sword.

I moved around the fire anyway.

"*I'm serious*." She got to her feet, moving away from me like my touch truly revolted her.

"I can keep you warm—"

"What part of *I would rather die* do you not understand?" Her hatred was palpable, like a steady drumbeat inside her heart. Her palm was up, like she would push me if I came too close.

"This is about survival, Harlow. There are no emotions in survival."

"I disagree. Survival is all about emotions—and my gut is telling me that you aren't human, that you're a monster I've never encountered before, and I would be stupid if I let you get close to me again."

We made it another night without an attack from a hungry yeti, and now it was time to find a way down. I stood at the edge and looked down, seeing that it was too steep in most places. The snow was an extra hazard, making it slippery on already questionable terrain. We would have to find small sections we could cross and then find the next section…even if it were miles away.

Harlow hadn't said a word to me since last night. She'd already hated me before that conversation, and despite the fact that I was trying to keep her alive, she hated me even more because of it.

"You see that section?" I pointed in the distance, where the slope down was minimal. "We'll cross there, then find the next spot that's safe. We'll keep doing that until we get to the bottom."

"That'll take forever."

"But we'll live."

We began the journey, finding different spots that were crossable, slowly moving down the mountain. When the afternoon arrived, the wind picked up, and then the clouds thickened and dumped snow. A blizzard was on the way, and being on the edge of a mountain was the most precarious place we could be.

We kept moving, but the wind blew even harder, making visibility poor and the path slippery.

I grabbed her hand and pulled her forward.

She twisted from my grasp. "What did I say about touching me?"

"You're going to fall."

"I don't need your help, asshole." She stomped past me to make a point, moving down the mountain on her own.

I came to her side, making sure she was close in case she lost her footing. Our surroundings were blurred by snow, so it was impossible to see the bottom. We would only know if we were there once the ground flattened.

We kept at it all day, still going even when there was barely any sunlight left in the sky, but I pushed on because I felt like we were close. It would be safer to stop and wait until morning, but I knew Harlow felt a million times worse than she looked…and she already looked half dead.

"This is the bottom." I looked out in the darkness, seeing the flat terrain of snow. It stretched for fifty feet before the darkness swallowed the view. "If we stay tighter against the wall, it'll protect us from the wind."

"I know a cave not far from here." She could barely speak with the chattering of her teeth. Her breathing was different too, like her lungs weren't working the way they should. "It's close to the original path of the cliffs."

"What does it look like?"

"The slit is sideways, so when you look at it head on… it looks like a crack. But—i-it's so dark now that I-I don't think we'll b-be able to see it."

"I can find it. Come on." I moved ahead through the snow, but when I looked behind me, she'd barely made any progress. Her body was finally giving out on her, after days and nights in the freezing temperatures.

I moved back and lifted her into my arms.

When she didn't issue a single protest, I knew how bad off she really was. I cradled her against my chest as I carried her forward, in the howling wind and swirling snow, searching for the cave she described in minimal detail. I could see in the dark, but without the assistance of sunlight, it was hard to understand my location, especially in a foreign land. Back at home, I'd be able to figure out my location based on vegetation alone, but this was a whole new place.

Thirty minutes later, I got lucky and found the crack in the stone. The entry was small, and I had to step in sideways to enter. I sidestepped several feet before I entered a small cave which held storage containers and bedrolls, like it was a pit stop used by travelers. "Harlow, I found it." When I looked down at her face, she was asleep in my arms, her skin pale like the snow I'd just marched through.

I placed her in a bedroll, covered her with all the blankets I could find, and then started a fire. The wind howled outside as the flames crackled, and because of the limited space inside, it warmed up quickly, feeling like a cabin in the woods.

I looked through the storage containers and found dried meat and fruit, along with assorted nuts and water. I didn't realize how tired I was until I was able to stop. Didn't realize that the cold had seeped into my bones until I thawed out. I lay on the stone beside her and fell asleep instantly, the flames like a lullaby my mother used to sing to me.

She slept through the morning and into the afternoon.

The storm had passed, and it was the perfect opportunity to head to the path and make it to the top of the cliffs to get to the ship she'd promised, but I feared if she didn't rest, her body would succumb to the ordeal she'd just endured. Most other humans would have perished on that journey, but by sheer will and stubbornness, she'd survived what would have killed most men. She was small and delicate in appearance, but her substance was as powerful as the steel of my blade.

When she woke up, color had returned to her cheeks. Her lips were pink once again, and her eyes weren't so dry and empty. The first thing she did was look at the fire, then she touched the pile of blankets stacked on top of her. She touched her own hand and then her cheek, probably feeling the warmth of her body temperature. Then she sat up and looked for me, finding me sitting against the wall across the small cave. "You found it."

"You would have died if I hadn't." I nodded to the container of food and water I'd put beside her. "Eat and drink. Once we get to the top, we won't have to worry about the cold anymore." I was used to the cold in Crescent Falls, used to the snow every day of the year. Perhaps that was why I was able to handle the elements exceptionally well, in addition to my cold blood.

She scarfed everything down, eating what I provided then digging for more.

"How did you know about this place?"

"My father showed it to me. He used it before I was born."

"When he was trying to take Delacroix back...makes sense."

She sat down with her snacks and ate as she looked at me. "So, you are from around here."

Just because I knew their history didn't mean I was a resident. "I've heard the story."

"Then you know my mother and father are people you don't fuck with."

"I told Rancor that his idea to overthrow your father was a stupid one."

"Does he still intend to do that now that you're returning me?"

I shrugged. "I'm not sure. He never shared all the details with me. We're allies, but I don't support his cause."

"Then why did you go to him in the first place?"

"I told you I needed something from him."

"And what could the Teeth offer you that no one else could?"

I couldn't explain it, not without providing information about myself.

"What was so important that you would capture an innocent person?"

I still said nothing.

When she got no information from me, she finished her food and water then got to her feet. "Let's go. I can't wait to be home."

We reached the path up the cliff and took it on foot. It would have been much easier on horseback, and I felt the burn in my thighs shortly after the ascent began. I expected to see soldiers looking for Harlow along the way, but to my surprise, nobody was there.

The higher up we went, the warmer it became, and Harlow started to shed her clothes on the hike. She gave me back my cloak, and she tied her sweater around her waist once she started to sweat.

We said nothing on the journey, focusing our energy on the hike.

I hadn't eaten since we'd left, so that would be my first activity once I was back. I'd find someone alone, someone I could drain and hide after I was done. If I let my prey live, someone would notice their bites, and soon rumors would start in the village. They had no idea what vampires were, but they knew what the Teeth were, so I would get labeled as one of them.

By the time we reached the top, I was so warm that I forgot how cold I'd been for the last week. I saw people nearby, but they were farmers about to take their harvest down to the bottom of the cliffs to deliver to the outpost. They didn't seem to notice her, more focused on their animals and their wagons.

We walked under the trees, and she moved toward the path that led to Delacroix.

"Where are you going?"

She stopped and looked at me over her shoulder. "Home?"

"You can go home after you get me my ship."

Her eyebrows furrowed before she walked back to me, the light back in her eyes now that she wasn't frozen solid. "How am I supposed to do that without speaking to my father?"

"I'm not stupid, Harlow. I know what your father will do to me."

Her eyes remained hard on my face. "I can't get you a ship without—"

"There are no ships in Delacroix. We need to travel to the port city, where you'll ask the steward to provide me with a ship and a crew—no questions asked. That was the deal, Harlow."

"I'm not doing that—"

"You bet your ass you are. You owe me."

"*I owe you?* Asshole, my parents probably think I'm dead right now. Or worse. The Teeth stripped me naked and tied me up like an animal. I almost died in that winter storm. It'll take us another week to travel to the port city, and if you think I'm going to let my parents suffer for another week, you're insane. They need to know that I'm okay."

"The sooner you get me that ship, the sooner you can tell them you're fine."

She shook her head. "No."

"*No?*"

"I don't even want to imagine how my parents are suffering right now. I get the impression you're some kind of loner who doesn't really have anyone, so you don't know what it's like to lose someone you love."

I almost laughed at the absurdity. "Sure…I have no idea what that's like."

Her eyes shifted back and forth between mine. "We go to Delacroix. I tell my parents I'm alright. Then I'll order your ship. You can travel to the port city and take off to wherever the fuck you want to go. Good riddance."

"The second I face your father, he'll kill me."

"He won't if I ask him not to."

"He'll be deaf in his rage."

"All he's going to care about is that I'm okay. You are not the priority, Aurelias."

"I don't buy that, sweetheart."

Anger rushed out of her like a billowing cloud of smoke. I noticed a subtle change in her eyes, a sharpening of daggers. "Don't call me that."

"We go to the port city."

"I'm going to Delacroix—and that's final. The only way that's not happening is if you force me. But you have no horse, no rope, and I doubt you have any more of whatever that was that put me out. All you have is that sword, and that's not going to earn my compliance. If you're that concerned about your neck, you should travel to the port city alone and steal your precious ship."

"I can't make the journey without a crew."

"Then kidnap the steward and force him—"

"*We made a deal.*"

"And I will honor that deal in Delacroix." Without waiting for my consent, she headed down the path toward the castle that was far away in the distance, past all the farmland that provided the meats and produce to feed its residents.

I stared at her retreating back, furious that this petite woman who was inferior to me in size and strength was calling the shots. "Harlow."

She turned back around.

"I want your word."

"I said I'll get you a ship—and I will."

"And?"

"My father won't kill you." She turned forward again and continued her walk. "Come on. I'm tired, hungry, and ready for a bath. A triple threat."

I detected no hint of a lie, no malice. When people lied, their expressions gave them away, and the same was true of their hearts. I could feel a surge of dread whenever someone tried to deceive me—and I didn't feel that when she spoke.

We approached the gate of Delacroix, and the second the guards spotted their princess, they started to blare the horn so the king and queen would hear it up at the castle. They didn't draw their swords on me, probably because she and I walked side by side like allies rather than enemies.

We walked up the hill toward the castle, the sunshine blazing hot and painful against my skin. We said nothing to each other, and I could feel the building emotion inside her chest, the invisible tears that she didn't shed, the anticipation of relieving her parents' fears that she was no longer in this world.

The queen appeared at the top of the stairs to the castle, dressed in her uniform and armor like she was ready for battle if she were called. She looked down at us, and even from this distance, I could see the overwhelming emotion on her face. She took off at a run, sprinting toward her daughter with the desperate need of a worried mother.

"Mama…" Harlow ran forward to meet her mother halfway, and they collided like two powerful boulders slamming into each other.

Her mother squeezed her tightly, breaking down into painful sobs as she held her. "Harlow…"

"I'm okay."

Her mother continued to cry as she held her, and the scene reminded me of my own mother's reaction when I'd been lost in the forest for several days. I'd gone there to hunt, but I fell and sprained my ankle, and I was stuck alone for several days and several nights, afraid my father would never find me. I was a boy at the time, so he carried me home in his arms, and when my mother saw me…she was delirious with relief. My father was vocal about his favorite son, but my mother truly loved each one of us equally.

"Are you okay?" Queen Rolfe pushed Harlow's hair out of her face as she cupped her cheeks.

"Just hungry."

The queen smiled through her tears and even released a chuckle. "Attagirl." Her arm circled her daughter's shoulders, and they walked together back to the castle.

I trailed behind, realizing that Harlow was right, that her mother's relief masked her need for revenge.

"Where's Father?" Harlow asked.

"He left yesterday to search for you. Hasn't returned."

"Is there a way we could send a missive?"

"I'll send word to HeartHolme. Hopefully they can get him the message."

We stopped in front of the castle, and Queen Rolfe only had eyes for her daughter, who had inherited her soft features and the color of her hair. I seemed to be forgotten—until Harlow looked at me.

The queen followed her gaze and stared at me, and instantly, that warmth was replaced by a coldness that rivaled the storm we'd just faced. But she said nothing, her sharp gaze piercing me like the sword in her belt. She didn't order the guards to take me away. Had no retaliation whatsoever.

Harlow was the one who stepped forward, and the pissed-off look on her face matched the swelling anger in her heart. "As Princess of Delacroix, I sentence you to a five-year imprisonment in our dungeon, punishment for your deceit and malice."

The guards started to converge, but my eyes were locked on hers, shocked that she'd lied to me—and did it so effortlessly. "All we have in this world is our word, and yours is now worthless."

"I won't kill you."

"But you promised me something—"

"You'll have your ship once your sentence is completed. My word is ironclad, but you failed to hash out the details. You feared my father, when you should have feared me. I'm my father's daughter—and I've inherited his vengeance, his rage, and his malice."

I let the guards take me, looking into her beautiful face with a mixture of anger and respect.

"Now you know exactly how I felt when you used me—like a fool." She gestured to the guards. "Take him away."

19

HARLOW

Once I had a shower and a full meal, I felt like myself again. My hair was soft and shiny, and the clothes I wore were clean and dry. Sunlight came through my open window, the comforts of home surrounding me after a cruel journey.

My mother tapped her knuckles against the open door before she stepped inside. "Feel better?"

"*A lot* better."

She sat on the couch beside me, her smile warm but her eyes broken. "I was so worried…" Her hand rested on mine.

I turned my palm and grabbed her fingers. "I know."

"Did he hurt you?"

"No."

"Did he...?" She didn't finish the question.

"No."

She breathed a sigh of relief, her eyes on the ground. "Then what did he want?"

"He made a deal with the Teeth. I was his bargaining chip."

"What did he want from them?"

"He wouldn't tell me."

"Why did he take you all the way down there, just to bring you back?"

"Rancor promised him a ship to return to his homeland but revoked it now that Father is watching the coast."

She gave a slight nod, her eyes still on the ground. "Good thing Uncle Ian spotted that black ship."

"Yes."

"Your father will be so happy to see you." She met my gaze again. "He was so strong when I told him the news, but I know he didn't want to be."

My heart broke thinking about the way his heart would have shattered into a million pieces. He was a man of few words, of few emotions, but he felt deeply when it came to Atticus and me. He looked at us in this special way…a way I couldn't describe.

"I sent Atticus a message. Once he receives it, he'll return with our army. General Henry and his men are at the bottom of the cliffs. I expected one of them to find you, not for you to walk back inside with your abductor."

"We didn't pass the soldiers because we moved through the mountains. It was the only way to escape the Teeth."

"Well, I'm grateful that man brought you back alive, at least."

"He's not a man…"

"Then what is he?"

"I have no idea." He wasn't Teeth. He wasn't Necrosis. I couldn't figure it out.

"Your father may know. He's seen a lot of things."

My thumb brushed her fingers.

"Are you okay?"

"I'm fine, Mother. Compared to all the horrible things that could have happened, it was a fairy tale."

She gave a nod. "I meant…are you okay with…what happened between you and that man?"

I held her gaze, unable to share my feelings like I normally did. I'd told her about Ethan. I'd told her about my first time. I told her everything—because she was my best friend. But this time…it was hard.

"I can tell he hurt you…based on the last things you said to him."

Our journey felt like a single day because I'd had no time to process everything that had happened. We were always together, bickering, fighting, detesting each other. "I should have been more suspicious. I'd never seen him around the village, and then all of a sudden, he shows up out of thin air…and I'm the only thing he's interested in. He's a very handsome man, so that was a red flag too."

"It's not your fault, sweetheart. Living a life of constant suspicion is no life at all. And he's not out of your league, if that's what you're implying."

"You're my mother. You have to say that."

"But I mean it. And I bet he would agree."

He was underneath the castle, locked up in the dungeon, the very dungeon where my grandfather was kept before my father killed him, and I wouldn't go down there to visit him. The next time I would see him would be in five years when he was released. "It's not like I can trust anything he says."

"I'm sorry that he hurt you." She patted my hand. "I can tell you really liked him."

And that made me feel even more foolish. "I did my best not to get attached, knowing it wasn't a long-term thing, but…it was hard not to." I'd only been with Aurelias a couple of times, and I masked my affection with distance because I knew I didn't want it to end. I'd never felt that level of heat with another man, never felt that throbbing connection. I didn't really know him because he was so closed off, but I wanted to know the rivers in his soul more than anything. "But that's over now. Time to move on."

My father still hadn't returned.

Now I worried for him the way he worried for me. He'd gone to the Teeth to negotiate my release, and I hoped it didn't claim his life. It was hard to get back into a routine when life was forever changed. The era of peace had officially ended.

Mother and I spent a lot of time together, and it seemed like she wanted to keep me in her sights all the time, like someone would take me all over again. But there was a distinct melancholy to her features, and I knew it was because she worried for my father.

We had breakfast together in the dining room, just the two of us because my father and brother were absent, and a guard entered. "Princess Harlow, you have a visitor who requests an audience."

I turned in my chair to regard him. "Who?"

"Ethan Knotworthy."

"He probably wants to see if you're okay," Mother said.

"I'm obviously okay if I'm home."

She sipped her coffee before she returned the cup to the saucer. "Ethan helped me figure out exactly what happened, so I think he deserves a moment of your time, Harlow."

"He was able to help you because he spied on me."

"Nonetheless, he cares."

"Alright." I rose to my feet.

The guard spoke again. "And the prisoner wishes to have a word with you."

My heart sank, hoping to never hear about him again. "His request is denied." I walked past the guard and headed outside, finding Ethan waiting for me in the courtyard. He sat on the stone that surrounded the fountain, and once he saw me coming, he jumped up to meet me.

He moved into my chest and hugged me, held me before I had a chance to do anything else. "I'm glad you're alright." He cupped the back of my head and pressed a kiss to my forehead, like I was still his.

The affection felt suffocating, so I quickly stepped back to get space.

"I was worried you wouldn't come back."

"You know me. I never let anyone push me around." I forced a smile.

He stared with his intense eyes, looking at me like it took all his strength not to cup my cheek and kiss me.

I crossed my arms over my chest to prevent the advance. "Thank you for helping my mother. I know it didn't lead to my rescue, but having some information was better than nothing."

He didn't acknowledge what I said. "How did you get back?"

I told him the entire story, that we returned for his ship.

"So, he's gone, then?"

"Actually, he's in the dungeon."

"Your mother was angry."

"No, I put him there. If he thinks he can steal me from my kingdom and use me as a bargaining chip without retaliation, he's an idiot."

"Spoken like a real queen."

"Spoken like my father's daughter."

He stared for a while, the silence growing uncomfortable because there was nothing more to say. "Maybe this isn't the best time, but...you know I would never hurt you like that. I would never use you like that. Why are you wasting time on men who don't give a damn about you when you know I would give my life for yours in the blink of an eye?"

"Ethan...you're so sweet."

"I'm only sweet to you. I hurt a lot of women in the past."

"I don't understand why you would even want me after the way I treated you."

"Because you're the one."

I dropped my gaze, uncomfortable with his unconditional affection. "Ethan..."

He moved in and cupped my face, giving me a kiss I wasn't prepared to receive. But it was a good kiss, the kind that warmed my cold lips, that made me feel valued rather than used.

But I pulled away anyway. "Ethan, I'm just not in the proper headspace right now."

His eyes were hurt, but he didn't make another advance. "After everything he did, you still have feelings for him?" His incredulity was audible.

"I—I'm still hurt." I couldn't describe it. I'd just thrown him in a prison underneath the castle as revenge for the way he'd hurt me, but kissing Ethan somehow felt like a betrayal though Aurelias and I never had expressed even the slightest commitment to each other. "And I guess it hurts…because it meant something to me."

"You were with me for months—and him a week."

"I know it doesn't make sense—"

"None, actually."

"Ethan—"

"He was going to hand you over to our enemies and only refrained because they didn't give him what he wanted. Let that sink in, Harlow."

"I understand—"

"I don't think you understand at all."

"I locked him up under the castle because I want nothing to do with him, but that doesn't mean my heart is ready to just move on, Ethan. It needs time to heal, to get over the betrayal. I don't think that's hard to understand. You need to stop chasing me because you're a man who shouldn't have to chase anyone."

"I'd much rather chase the one woman I want than settle for your replacement."

I stared at the garden that surrounded us, avoiding his penetrating gaze, the gaze that was so hard it could chisel his sculptures. "I should go."

A flash of disappointment moved across his eyes, but he kept it locked behind his lips. "I'm glad you're home safely, Harlow. You know where to find me…if you change your mind."

The guard informed us that Atticus had returned with the army, so Mother and I ran outside to meet my brother.

He pulled his helmet off his head as he walked to us, his mouth wide with a grin. He handed the helmet to one of the nearby soldiers and walked up to me, looking more like Father than when he left, with the armor that fit his powerful body perfectly. He moved right into me and embraced me, lifting me from the ground as he hugged me in a way he never had before. "I was so relieved when I got Mother's message." He squeezed me before he returned me to the ground. "You're okay?"

"Not a scratch."

He embraced Mother next. "Where's Father?"

"He still hasn't returned," she said solemnly. "But I'm sure he'll be back soon. We sent a letter to Heart-Holme to tell your grandmother that Harlow is home safe. I know she'll relay the message to your father."

Atticus continued his stare, his fears not alleviated. "I should take the army down—"

"*No.*" She raised her voice slightly, unintentionally. She calmed herself before she continued. "Your father is protected by two fierce dragons. I'm sure he's alright—and I can't part with another child right now."

"Then we should still send the army—"

"I can't deplete Delacroix of its forces and leave it unprotected, not when I don't know the circumstances."

"We can't do nothing—"

"Give him another day," she said. "The Teeth are defenseless against two dragons. He just left before Harlow arrived, so we need to give him more time. Once he discovered that Harlow wasn't with the Teeth, I'm sure he flew to HeartHolme to plan his next move, which means he'll receive my letter any moment now."

That seemed to be enough to assuage Atticus because he didn't protest further.

"Princess Harlow?" A guard appeared at my side. "I'm sorry to interrupt, but the prisoner wishes to speak with you."

"I already denied that request."

"He says if you don't want to break your word, you should speak with him."

I had no idea what that meant. "I'll be there shortly."

The guard retreated.

Atticus stared at me, his eyebrows furrowed in consternation the way Father's did.

"It's a long story…" I told him the tale.

"Why is he alive?" he demanded. "He should be killed for his crimes, not imprisoned."

"He did get me back safely—"

After he took you.

"But if I'd escaped on my own, I would have died on the journey. He kept me alive. And he did get me out of there. I don't think death is a fair punishment."

"Father is the most just king there ever was, and I know he would disagree."

"It's over now," I said. "Let's move on."

I made it downstairs to the dungeons, which were all empty because we hadn't had a prisoner in a very long time. Crime was limited in Delacroix because everyone was well-fed and housed. There was no reason to steal. Domestic abuse and rape were also rare, because my father had a zero-tolerance policy for such crimes. Perpetrators wouldn't end up in the dungeon anyway.

There was no natural light this far below the castle, so the sconces on the walls were the only form of light in this dark place. My heart raced as I approached the cell in the corner, dreading the moment I had to look at the man who'd broken my heart before I even had a chance to give it to him.

He sat against the wall, one arm propped on his knee, the back of his head resting against the stone. His eyes were locked on mine, dark like saturated soil. There should be hostility and rage in that gaze, but instead, there was quiet defeat.

The guard placed a chair for me to sit and then moved back to the doorway where he could watch us, out of earshot.

I sat down and continued to stare at Aurelias, seeing the way his appearance had changed in the last two days. His skin was paler than I remembered, his eyes were bloodshot, and he somehow looked thinner. His armor and weapons had been taken away, so he sat there in a shirt and trousers, the pale skin of his arms tight over the cords of his veins.

He continued his quiet stare.

"You got me down here to give me the silent treatment?"

"Tell him to leave." He nodded to the guard near the stairs.

"I'm not an idiot, Aurelias."

"We need to speak in private, and I don't want a servant to overhear this conversation."

I didn't oblige and continued to sit there.

"If I could break through these iron bars, I would have done it already."

After I released a sigh, I turned to the guard and gave him a nod.

He moved up the stairs, and then his footsteps disappeared.

"If you leave me in here, I'm going to die."

"Misery can't kill you."

"Misery isn't the culprit." He got to his feet and walked to the bars, his arms sliding through and resting on the iron center bar. "If you want to keep your word by sparing my life, then you need to let me go."

"You can't manipulate me."

"I'm not manipulating you—"

"Nothing in here will kill you."

"But what I need to survive isn't here. So, therefore, I will die."

"Like meds? Are you ill?"

"Something like that."

"Then tell me what you need, and I'll get it for you."

He rubbed his palms together and gave a quiet sigh. "I can't do that."

"Because you're lying—"

"Because I can't tell you what I need to survive."

"There's no scenario in which I let you walk out of there, Aurelias. So, either tell me what you need or die." I got to my feet, ready to leave this pointless conversation.

He didn't say a word, but he expressed his anger with the tightness of his clenched jaw. "I'm sorry that I hurt you, but how many times do I have to say that it wasn't personal? Because it really wasn't—"

"And that's exactly the problem."

"I didn't want to do this—"

"But you did."

"You're one petty woman, aren't you?"

"If I were a man, would you call me petty? If some woman seduced you—"

"I didn't seduce you, sweetheart. You seduced *me*."

I came closer to the bars, arms crossed over my chest, refusing to grow weak for those dark eyes.

"All I had to do was drug you and take you. But then you wanted me, and I wasn't going to say no to that."

"You came on to me—"

"Because I knew you wanted me."

"How?" I snapped.

He bowed his head and cracked his knuckles. "I just did."

"You just did…"

He lifted his head and looked at me again. "And then I fucked you, and all I wanted to do was fuck you again, and it turned into this addiction…"

"But then you kidnapped me."

"Again, I didn't *want* to do it."

"But you did. You took me to the Teeth so I would be killed, and the only reason you got me out of there was because I unexpectedly became more useful to you than they were. I'm alive right now because you need a ship."

He stared at me, his jawline tight as he clenched his teeth again.

"I don't feel bad that you're in here. And I certainly don't feel bad for being the one who put you here."

He straightened to his full height, sliding his arms onto different rungs. He stared at the floor for a long time, looking pissed off. "Look, that's not the whole story."

"What's not the whole story?"

He wouldn't look at me, eyes still on the floor. "When I made the deal with the Teeth, they said they would only use you as leverage then let you go. But when I arrived, they had changed their plans. They would use you as bait to get your father, but you would be dead before he even arrived. And…they would do things to you in the meantime." After a pause, he lifted his chin and looked at me again. "They still offered me a ship, but on a different coast. I got you out of there because I wasn't going to let them do that to you."

My expression remained hard as I stared, but my heart raced with the speed of a galloping horse. My eyes searched his for sincerity, for a sign of the truth or a lie. "You expect me to believe that?"

"It's the truth—so I would hope so."

"If this is the truth, why didn't you say something before?"

"Because."

"*Because what?*"

He stared, rubbing his palms together as he gave a loud sigh.

"You're so full of it—"

"Because I don't give a fuck about anyone, and I didn't want to give a fuck about you." He stepped back from the bars and moved away, looking at the stone wall he'd rested against when I walked in.

"You would rather me think you're a heartless asshole?"

"Prefer it, actually." He continued to stare at the back wall, his broad shoulders strong, his back rising and falling with his frustrated breaths. "It was fucked up that I mislead you and took you, and I understand there will be retribution for that, but I did also bring you back, and that fact is important." He turned back around and looked at me again, but he didn't approach the bars. "I only have a few days, at most."

I couldn't deny the fact that he didn't look like himself. It was like he hadn't eaten in weeks.

He waited for me to speak, his eyes intense, visceral.

"Harlow." He moved back to the bars, his arms resting on the center bar again. "Let me go."

"You made my family suffer."

"I didn't want to."

"But you did it—"

"Trust me, I had no choice."

"How? How did you have no choice?"

"Harlow—"

"If you want me to let you go, no more secrets." I faced him, arms tight around my waist, feeling the attraction

I wished would fade. He looked close to the grave, but he was somehow just as sexy as the first time I saw him. "I mean it."

He bowed his head for a moment, releasing another heavy sigh. Then he straightened his neck and gave me a cold look. "I came to your land because I needed a special venom from the Teeth, a type of venom that would save a lot of people. They agreed to give it to us—but only if I agreed to kidnap the Princess of Delacroix. You don't know me that well, so you'll have to take my word for it when I say kidnapping people is not in my regular job description."

"Why venom?"

"The specifics of the serum are not pertinent to our situation."

"I want to know everything—"

"*Too bad*," he snapped. "I told you everything that directly affects you. Stop being greedy. I don't pry into your life and your affairs, even though I've wanted to. Now you understand why I was in your lands, what I was doing here, and how it relates to you. Let me go—or let me die."

Our relationship was based on a lie, a malicious deceit, but for some reason, I believed him. I believed that he wasn't like the Teeth, that he wished me no harm, and that he did have a heart, even though he tried desperately not to.

"Harlow."

The guard came downstairs again. "I apologize for the interruption, Princess Harlow, but King Rolfe has returned. His dragon has been sighted in the distance."

A jolt of relief rushed through me, relief so potent I released a gasp. It made me forget about Aurelias, made me forget the entire conversation we'd just had. I left the cell and moved to the stairs—forgetting about the man I was leaving behind.

20

HUNTLEY

I sat in my mother's study as the fire burned in the hearth.

She sat on her throne and stared at me.

Ian sat in the other chair across the room, his eyes on the floor like he couldn't focus.

"What does this mean, Huntley?" Several moments of silence had just passed after I'd told her about Harlow. It pulled her deep under the surface, made her drown in misery just the way it did with me. There were no words of condolence—because it was impossible to console a terrified parent.

I stared at the fire, my lungs aching every time I took a breath. "It means war is upon us. A war that we can't prepare for, because we don't know the enemy." I continued to stare at the flames, but all I saw was my daughter's face. I hadn't slept. Wouldn't be able to sleep for a very long time. "A couple decades of peace is too short for us to enjoy. I expected a much longer period of serenity than this."

"You speak as if we've already lost the war," my mother said.

"The Teeth wouldn't challenge us unless they were certain they could defeat us. Whoever their enemy is, I know they're formidable."

"We'll need to send dragons to the east as scouts," Ian said. "We need to figure out what we're up against."

"We only have so many dragons," Mother said.

"We have no other choice," Ian said. "There's no other way to access the east—unless we travel by ship."

"And that's even more dangerous," I said.

"We must use the dragons," Ian said. "And do our best to stay out of sight."

Mother continued to look at me, her stare piercing. "We'll gather what information we can. In the meantime, we prepare our army, ask for volunteers. Elora will need to make new armor for the remaining dragons."

"That's assuming they agree to fight for us," Ian said. "Which they may not."

"We rescued them," Mother said. "Have given them land and peace these last twentysomething years. They owe us."

"But we did that without expectation," I said. "Ian is right. I'd rather have a dragon that wants to fight for us than one that is obligated. I know Storm would give his life for mine—and that's because he wants to."

Mother nodded in agreement.

I'd come to this conclusion almost immediately, and I knew it was unlikely I would have another option. "Depending on what we discover, I'll travel to the east alone—and offer myself in exchange for Harlow."

Both of them looked at me.

"Ian." I looked at my brother. "I'd like you to be King of Kingdoms if that happens. Ivory will be unable to lead under those circumstances. So will my son and daughter."

Ian lifted his chin and looked at me, his face devoid of emotion.

Mother didn't object, because she would do the same for her sons.

And Ian didn't object either—because he had a daughter of his own. He finally gave a nod. "Let's gather our information first. Perhaps we'll find another way."

21

IAN

Huntley wanted to be alone, to sit by the fire and stare into its depths as he thought about the fate of his daughter. I went to the pub and drank alone, thinking about my niece whom I loved like my own daughter.

There was nothing we could do at this moment—and that made it worse. We were powerless. We had no leads. Had no idea what we were up against. We couldn't just draw our swords and attack.

I left the pub and walked to the cottage that didn't belong to me. I'd drunk a little too much, and that was probably why I had the courage to do this. The torch burned above the doorway, the only sensation of heat in the cold darkness. I banged my fist against the door harder than I meant to.

A moment later, Avice opened the door, her eyes guarded at my presence.

I stared, loving the soft angles of her face, the beauty of her eyes. The first time I saw her, I knew she was the most beautiful woman I'd ever seen. And I still thought she was the most beautiful woman I'd ever seen.

She kept one hand on the door, ready to shut it in my face if I said the wrong thing.

Now that I was face-to-face with her, the words weren't there.

"I can tell you're drunk."

I should have stayed sober, because we officially lived in a time when an attack could come at any moment. An enemy could arrive on our doorstep, and I wouldn't be able to hold my sword steady. "Yeah."

"Go home, Ian." She started to shut the door.

"Wait." My hand planted against the door and forced it open. "I need you right now."

"That's not my problem—"

"Harlow has been taken."

That was all it took to change her attitude. Her hand slid down the edge of the door, and she inhaled a breath of despair. "Who took her?"

"The Teeth."

"Then why are you on my doorstep—"

"Because they fled to the east. They're under the mountains, and we have no idea where. There's nothing we can do until they're on the other side."

"What—what does this mean?"

"That the Teeth have allies—and we're at war." I crossed the threshold and moved into the cottage, forcing her to back up. I closed the door behind me and approached her, circling my arms around her waist and pulling her flush against me. My chin rested on her head, and I closed my eyes—because it felt so damn good.

I couldn't remember the last time I'd held her like this.

She didn't push me off, but she didn't reciprocate the affection either.

I didn't drop my hold, because I knew it would never come again.

Then her arms circled my waist, and she held me back.

My eyes clenched to contain the tears.

We stayed that way in the middle of the dark living room, the candles our only light. It was warm, like the fire that had been lit a few hours ago had been enough to warm the house through the night.

How could something so horrible bring me something so good?

Minutes later, she pulled away.

She had to leave first, because I was never going to leave. I would have stayed like that forever.

"How are you going to get her back?"

"I don't know."

"Huntley doesn't have a plan?"

"We're going to send scouts to the east to see what we discover. Depending on that information, Huntley may give himself up in exchange. There may be no other option. They wouldn't have taken Harlow unless she would be useful to them, and the only way she's useful politically is because her father is the King of Kingdoms."

"This can't be happening."

It was the worst nightmare of my life.

"Ivory..."

"She's a mess."

"And Huntley..."

"He's a different kind of mess."

She rubbed her arms, like a draft had come from nowhere and made her shiver. "I—I can't believe this has happened."

"Neither can I."

"We've lived at peace for so long..."

"I know." The best decades of my life. I'd felt incomplete until I'd met Avice, until we'd had our daughter, until life had started to make sense. My mother preferred Huntley to me, but I knew Avice picked me when she could have had any other man she wanted.

"You—you don't think it's Necrosis?"

"They were all slain. The Three Kings were executed."

She gave a nod, but her eyes didn't look convinced. "Then who else could their allies be?"

"I don't know. The world is a vast place, and we really don't know much about it." We'd stuck to our continent, which was already enough work to maintain.

"I know Huntley will get her back." She said it to herself more than anything.

I gave a nod, knowing I'd probably lose my brother in the end, but I wouldn't talk him out of it. If this were my daughter, I would do exactly the same thing. "Yeah." Even in sadness, Avice was the most beautiful creature I'd ever seen. My body was a natural furnace, but without her beside me, I felt ice-cold. Every mattress I slept on felt like a pile of rocks when she wasn't there.

Her eyes met mine, feeling the intensity of my stare.

My mind was in a haze because of all the scotch I'd drunk, but I was fully aware of my actions—of the fact that I wanted to sleep in her bed tonight. It took terror and booze to work up the courage to come here after weeks of not speaking, and now I was there, imagining the desperation written all over my face. "I—I'm broken." I hadn't prepared a speech before I arrived, and maybe that was why she listened to me. "My world fell apart when I lost you, but now...it's even worse. There are no words to comfort my brother, and as much as I love Harlow like my own, a part of me is grateful it's not Lila...and that makes me feel like the biggest scumbag on the continent." Tears welled in my eyes that I didn't feel until they started to fall, hot drops down my cheeks.

Her eyes instantly mirrored mine, wet with a sheen of emotion, bubbling up to the surface immediately. "I feel the same way." She came closer to me, her palms cupping my cheeks, giving me affection that I craved every day we were apart. Then she rested her forehead against mine.

I closed my eyes as I simmered in the throbbing connection between us, the love that had still survived my treason. She claimed she didn't want me anymore, but when I showed up on her doorstep, drunk and broken, she took me in with open arms. She cried when I cried. Her heart finally broke free of its prison and formed wings.

We still had a chance.

I knew it was wrong to take advantage of the situation for my own gain, but talking and pleading hadn't dented the armor around her heart. Tragedy was the only thing strong enough to make it through—so I wielded it like a sledgehammer.

My arm tightened around her waist, and I pulled her body flush against mine as I closed the minimal distance between our mouths and kissed her. It was a gentle landing, just the press of our lips. I tested her reaction, not wanting to advance too hard and lose her in the process.

But she didn't pull away.

I kissed her again. Felt her upper lip between mine. Kissed her bottom lip.

She still didn't push me away.

My hand cradled the back of her head, and I deepened the kiss, opening my mouth and feeling hers reciprocate. I turned my head and slipped her my tongue, feeling hers dance with mine. I moaned into her mouth when I knew this was real, that I wasn't alone in my bedroom with my fingers around my length and my eyes closed. I was kissing my wife—and she was kissing me back.

Her arms slid over my shoulders and around my neck, her fingertips sliding into the back of my hair. She rose on her tiptoes to meet my kiss, and after a few minutes, we became the fire that heated the room.

She was in her nightdress, so I gathered the material and lifted it up her body, revealing the tits I hadn't seen in months. I felt like a teenager who got to see boobs for the first time, and I stared a little too long before I kissed her again, my fingers hooking in her panties before pulling them over her ass.

The last woman I'd been with had happened months ago, and I'd felt so guilty about it that I didn't enjoy it. The last time I'd been with Avice had been even longer, so for me, it felt like a dry spell that had lasted an eternity.

She started to take off my clothes, removing the top of my uniform to expose my naked chest. She hesitated the way I did when I saw her tits, like she'd forgotten just how muscular I was, how my chest was thick like the walls that protected this city.

My mouth caught hers again, and I grabbed her ass as I kissed her, all my desire pouring out like lava from a volcano. I wanted her—so fucking badly. I felt her loosen my trousers and get my boxers down, my rock-hard dick exposed.

I kicked my boots off before I lifted her from the floor and took her into the bedroom down the hall, the bedroom I'd never seen before. The sheets were rumpled like she'd been sleeping when I knocked on the door. I dropped her on top then moved between her thighs, bringing our bodies close together, my sex touching hers for the first time in gods knew how long.

She was so warm…so smooth.

I should slow this down, but I was so pent up and desperate that I guided myself between her lips and sank, pushing past her body's initial resistance and sliding nice and slow. The groan that escaped my lips was long and drawn-out, feeling her tightness like it was the first time.

She moaned with me, her eyes burning like flames.

I stopped when there was nowhere else to go, fully buried in my wife, reunited with her, body and soul. Anxious and desperate, I wanted to fuck her like a whore I'd paid for the night, but I forced myself to slow down and treasure every moment we shared. I folded her underneath me and brought us close together, kissing her as I rocked into her, making love to the only woman I ever loved.

She said my name, a whisper on her lips, nails deep in my back like stakes buried in the ground. "Ian…"

The sound of her voice was ingrained in my mind, so I could hear it in my head all the time, recreate it when I wanted to hear it most. I pictured her saying my name many times, in my darkest fantasies when I imagined she was still mine. "Baby…"

I hadn't had a good night's sleep like that since…I'd lost her.

I opened my eyes, the morning light coming through the window and stretching across the bed. Her beautiful skin glowed in the warmth. She was on her side facing the window, still asleep.

It took all my strength not to kiss her.

I moved closer to her, pressed my chest to her back, and hooked my arm over her stomach. My face rested against her hair, and I smelled her, remembering when I got to do this every single day.

We lay that way for a long time then she started to stir, stretching her body and grinding her ass right against my hard dick without realizing it. She took a deep breath then let it out slowly, her eyes opening to the sunlight right on her face.

"Morning." I pressed a kiss to the back of her shoulder.

"Morning..."

"It's going to be a beautiful day." I looked at the light coming through the window as the peace settled on my shoulders. I hadn't felt this calm, this grounded, in a long time. For the first time, I appreciated the little things, the softness of sheets, the warmth of sunshine on a cold day, a quiet house because it was just the two of us.

She left my hold and got to her feet, stunning in her nakedness, her sexy curves breathtaking. She bent over to grab her nightdress from the floor, and I felt my dick twitch when I got a perfect view of everything. There were stretch marks on her tummy from Lila—and I found those the sexiest of all. She covered herself with the dress, but the image was seared into my mind. "I'm going to make coffee."

"Alright." I watched her go as I stayed in bed, remembering the mornings she would wake up the house with her cooking. She'd usually make pancakes and bacon for us. Lila and I would fight over the crunchiest pieces of meat.

I smelled the coffee moments later and walked into the living room, my clothes on the floor where I'd left them. I put on my boxers before I tossed the wood into the fireplace and got it started. The flames came to life and immediately brought warmth to the cottage. When I walked to the kitchen counter, I saw the mug waiting for me, black and steaming.

She ran her fingers through her hair before she took a drink, gorgeous first thing in the morning, when her eyes were rested.

I wanted to pack her things and bring them back to the castle that very morning, but I knew I shouldn't rush it. She'd probably want to take it slow, have dinner a few times, work on the relationship before we were back to our marital bliss.

I noticed she hadn't looked at me yet. "Everything alright?"

"Yeah. Just waking up."

My arm slid around her waist, and I pulled her close, kissing her on the mouth. But unlike last night, there wasn't much warmth to it. Her lips were stiff and cold. I pulled away to look at her face, to see the way she avoided my look again. "Baby?"

She looked down into her coffee.

Now I stared at her face…and saw the look of regret.

"Ian…"

My heart shattered into a million pieces.

"Last night was…just a one-time thing."

It took all my strength to keep my composure, not to scream and throw things, not to break down into tears.

"It was just a moment, and that moment has passed." When I didn't say anything, she found the courage to look at me. "We were both upset…and needed the comfort."

"You still love me, Avice."

"Of course I still love you—"

"*Then be with me.* You can't make love to me and act like it meant nothing."

She released a deep sigh. "I'm not saying it meant nothing, Ian."

"If you even want me to touch you, that means you must be over what happened."

"Over what happened?" she asked. "You mean you screwing another woman? No, I'll never be over that."

I probably shouldn't have even mentioned it, even though we were both thinking it. "We can't have a night like that unless we're both still in the same place emotionally. Even if it was just for comfort, that's not how you would have wanted comfort if you were still hurt. You still want this, but now that you've had it and it's fucking beautiful, you're scared to get hurt again."

Her eyes turned cold. "And do you blame me?"

"Avice, you need to forgive me—"

"I'm required to do no such thing."

"I've forgiven you for pushing me away. I'm ready to start over—"

"Pushing someone away isn't the same thing as cheating on them."

Now we were yelling at each other like a couple on the brink of divorce. A beautiful night had come at a price—heartbreak. I took a moment to breathe, to try to figure out a way to navigate through this. "Avice...I'm insanely in love with you. I want to be a family again. Please...just give me another chance."

She looked at her coffee again, dismissing me. "I'll always love you, Ian. But I'll never trust you again. Please...just go." She kept her head down, like she didn't want to watch me grab my things and leave.

Frozen to the spot, I didn't know what to do. "Avice...please."

"I'm sorry, Ian. Please...just go."

I returned to the castle, feeling worse than when I'd left. I stopped by Huntley's bedchambers, but he wasn't there. I wouldn't tell him what happened with Avice, not when there were more important things to worry about right now. I went to my mother's chambers afterward, finding her sitting on her throne.

"Ian." She rose to her feet in a hurry. "Where have you been?"

"Why? What's wrong?"

"Huntley left for Delacroix. We got a letter from Ivory saying that Harlow had returned."

I closed my eyes as the breath left my lungs. "Fuck, that's good news."

"Your brother left in the middle of the night. We tried to find you, but you weren't in your bedchambers." There was accusation in that stare—hard accusation.

I'd boasted about my conquests as a young man, but after I found Avice, I never shared those details with anyone—not even my brother. Out of respect for her, I wouldn't do it now, even though she'd just carved me with a butter knife.

"Spending your nights at the whorehouse won't repair your marriage, Ian."

My mother would never speak to Huntley that way, and it was another moment when she showed her preference for him over me. She did it all the time unconsciously, and it never improved, despite my dedication to HeartHolme. "I wasn't at the whorehouse."

"Then where were you?"

"My business is my own, Mother," I snapped. "I'm relieved that Harlow is alright. What else did the letter say?"

She recoiled slightly at my harshness but didn't address it verbally. "The letter was written in a hurry and said nothing more."

"Does Huntley want me to join him?"

"We need to prepare HeartHolme for war. If your brother needs you, he'll send word."

I nodded, feeling a relief so soothing it combated the pain Avice had just caused me. My mind had worked frantically to imagine all the horrible things happening to Harlow, and it was enough to make me collapse and never rise again. I should return to Avice and tell her the news, but I wasn't ready to face her...not yet.

I sat at a table alone in the pub, eating my pot roast with a loaf of bread. The booze hadn't worn off until a few hours ago, so I skipped it tonight. Now that war was brewing, I needed to be prepared for anything—like a breach of our gates.

Sometimes I received interested stares from the barmaidens and other girls, but I averted my gaze and pretended they didn't exist. There was only one woman I wanted, and a beautiful night still wasn't enough to make her take me back.

General Macabre walked inside the pub, not wearing his uniform and armor because he was off duty for the night. He was in charge of our armed forces, following my orders as the steward. My mother had stepped down some time ago due to her age, and the title had been passed to me. Despite the fact that he served me, we rarely spoke.

His eyes found mine, and he approached my table.

I wasn't in the mood for conversation, especially about the threat that loomed over the continent, but he dropped into the chair across from mine anyway. He was still and quiet, and the look he gave me was lethal.

I had no idea what had provoked his hostility, but I stared back with my own wrath. "Do you have a problem, General?"

He was ten years younger than me, had been younger than me during the war with Necrosis, but he'd moved up in the ranks because of his skill with the blade and his unparalleled intellect. My mother had promoted him, and I agreed with that suggestion. His stare was still furious. "Stay away from Avice."

He spoke very clearly, so I understood every word he said, but I was paralyzed on the spot because I didn't comprehend a word of it. I didn't speak, the horrible truth too much to bear.

"She's moved on—and so should you."

I'd met foes on the battlefield, held the best poker face in the game while they threatened to kill everyone I loved, and that was much easier to handle than this. I tried so hard to appear calm, to make my breathing normal rather than ragged, to hide how deep that blade just went into my ribs.

He got to his feet, prepared to leave now that the message was relayed. "You're the reason that marriage ended. Now be a man and give her the divorce."

22

HUNTLEY

The instant Storm dropped to the earth, I was on my feet and running past the gate into the city. I ran up the hill and approached the castle, expecting to see my wife and children, but I flew so fast and ran so hard that I probably beat the messenger.

I entered the castle doors and gave a scream. "Harlow!"

My daughter appeared a moment later, running up the stairs that led to the underground parts of the castle.

I nearly burst into tears at the sight of her.

"Father." With her dark hair flowing behind her as she ran in her white dress, she came to me, eyes identical to mine. Like the child who used to run into my arms when I was gone for the afternoon, she headed straight to me.

My arms caught her and squeezed her to me, my hand supporting the back of her head like she was still a toddler. All the emotions I'd buried inside my hard chest came to the surface as I held my firstborn, my only daughter, and I closed my eyes to keep those tears contained. But my breathing was impossible to control, uneven and rough.

I held my daughter like it was the last time and I was on my deathbed.

She let me hold her as long as I wanted, didn't try to pull away, didn't say a word to me.

We remained that way for a long time, the world quiet around us, everything right once more.

When I opened my eyes, I saw Ivory standing a distance away with Atticus at her side. I finally released my daughter and pulled back, looking down into her beautiful face. She was exactly as I remembered, her skin aglow with light, her eyes soft rather than hard, her smile gentle. There were a lot of things I wanted to say, but they wouldn't come out.

"I'm okay." She grabbed my forearm, even though she couldn't feel my skin through the vambrace. "Not a scratch." Her eyes shifted back and forth between mine, handling me like I was so fragile I would crumble at the slightest touch. She seemed to understand all my pain and suffering, even though she couldn't possibly understand a parent's love for their child. But that was my daughter—so damn smart.

I had a million questions to ask, a million things to say, but I was paralyzed by her looking back at me. Trapped in the darkness of my thoughts, the most horrible fears had come to me, fears so strong I'd wanted to take my life just to make them stop. So I just looked at her, seeing my daughter stare back at me with the eyes I gave to her.

She understood I needed another minute to look at her, to let my brain understand that she was truly here, that this wasn't a dream created by too much scotch. She moved into my chest and hugged me again.

My arms circled her, and I rested my chin on her head, staring at the floor, remembering the days when she used to fit in the crook of my arm. She'd wake up in the middle of the night crying, and to give Ivory a break since she was pregnant with my son, I would take Harlow, hold her in a single arm as I sat at my desk and waited for her to fall asleep. I wished she were that little again...so I could hold her and keep her safe.

When Harlow pulled away, Ivory approached, her eyes swimming with the same emotions. "Our babies are safe." She said it only to me, speaking quietly so our children wouldn't know that we still referred to them as infants even though they were grown adults.

I pulled her into me and kissed her on the forehead. "You alright, baby?"

"I was worried."

"I'm home. Our children are safe. Let your worries fade."

She moved away so she could reach my gaze. "I would take that advice...if we weren't at war."

I chose to bury my head in the sand when it came to most aspects surrounding Harlow. It was just easier that way. I did my duty in raising her to be a good person, but I also raised her to be smart and strategic, to demand what she wanted rather than settle for an attenuated version of it. I trained her in the sword, to protect herself against her foes, to reign as the greatest queen that ever lived.

But she was also a beautiful woman, and that was something I couldn't change.

I sat at the head of the dining table, the place where we had breakfast together every morning, Ivory with Atticus beside her, Harlow on my right. I wanted to treasure the fact that she was safe for a moment longer rather than dive into the details of her capture, but I had no other choice. "When I questioned the Teeth about the ship, they lied right to my face about their involvement, and I believed them. When your mother told me you'd been captured, Uncle Ian and I returned to set their kingdom on fire—but the kingdom was abandoned."

Harlow stiffened at the knowledge, her eyes widening slightly.

Ivory's expression didn't change, but I knew the news provoked her. "Then where are they?"

"There's nowhere to hide on the continent, so I suspect they've traveled underground to the east. Since the war ended, they've been digging...and digging. The tunnel must now be complete—and they've made friends on the other side."

"What kinds of friends?" Harlow asked.

I gave a curt shake of my head. "No idea, but I'm sure I'll find out soon..."

"Dragons can reach the east," Atticus said. "Perhaps they can find a route around or through the mountains. If there is no way, we have the fleet of ships."

"Why are we certain we're at war?" Ivory asked. "Perhaps the Teeth have fled from our retribution."

I looked at my wife. "They took Harlow for a reason, and there's only one reason they would provoke my wrath." Now I turned to my daughter, reaching the topic I'd dreaded since the moment I'd returned. "Tell me everything—without details."

Harlow immediately flicked her eyes away, just as uncomfortable as I was. "Aurelias drugged me and took me to the bottom of the cliffs by wagon. Once we were down there, we rode by horseback to the Teeth—"

"Why didn't you fight or flee?"

"I did many times," she said defensively. "But Aurelias isn't human."

"He's one of the Teeth." I'd already assumed this, although I couldn't understand how my daughter wouldn't have realized that.

"No," she said. "I'm not sure what he is. He's faster than anyone I've ever seen. His sword is made of black steel, something else I've never seen. He anticipates moves before they happen…like he knows they're coming."

I hung on to every word, unable to identify a being with those distinctive characteristics.

"We arrived at the Teeth, and he handed me over. They put me in a cell, and I was there less than an hour before Aurelias returned and broke me out. We had to climb the cliff to make it to the mountains…and made the return journey that way. Fuck, it was cold."

"Why would he release you immediately after handing you over?" I asked, the story not making sense.

"At the time, he said it was because the Teeth denied him the ship he was promised, so he asked if I would provide him with one if he saved me," she said. "I said yes. But then he later told me he did it because they said they were going to kill me...and he couldn't let that happen."

"How did you get him a ship?"

"I haven't yet," she said. "I put him in the dungeon as punishment for what he did."

I stared at my daughter, but I no longer saw her face. All I saw was the edge of my sword slicing through bone. Rage like I'd never known exploded through me, and I was on my feet so fast I knocked the chair back.

"Father, no." Harlow got to her feet. "I promised I wouldn't kill him."

"And I made no such promise." I left the dining table and headed to the door.

"Father, I know you're angry right now." She grabbed me by the arm and tried to drag me like she did as a child. "But I promised him I wouldn't kill him—"

I twisted out of her grasp. "Ivory. Atticus."

"Nooooo!"

Atticus grabbed his sister, and Ivory helped.

Harlow's screams followed me all the way down the hall. "Stop! Father, stop!"

I made it to the main part of the castle and then the staircase, descending to the bottom where the dungeons were tucked underneath the castle, prisoners never allowed to see the light of day.

I stepped into the dungeon and found him in the cage in the corner, leaning against the wall with his ankles and arms crossed. "Unlock it," I barked at the guard without even looking him in the face.

I approached the bars and looked into the cage, seeing the man stare back at me, not a shred of fear in his youthful face. He was smug—just as I expected him to be. I stared as the guard went to the cabinet to retrieve the key.

The man stared back, like he knew exactly who I was and the reason for my visit. "That's why Harlow's screaming."

I couldn't hear her at all. "Say her name again, and I'll torture you first."

The guard came over and fumbled with the key.

"I assumed you would interrogate me," he said, far too calm for someone about to be executed. "Seems like a waste, considering I worked directly with the Teeth."

The guard fumbled the key again, terrified of the tension between the two of us. He finally got the cell unlocked and swung the door forward.

He kept his position against the wall.

The dungeon was small, too small for my blade to swing around without hitting bars. So I removed my sword and handed it to the guard before I pulled out my dagger instead and walked in.

Now, he straightened, facing me as an enemy, though he had no weapon.

"Lock the door behind me," I ordered.

The guard turned the key, and the chain clanked against the metal bars.

He watched me.

I gripped the dagger, the blade pointing to the floor, wondering what I would go for first. I made my move, slicing the blade across his throat.

He ducked at the perfect time and moved to the other wall of the cell. "I didn't want to do it. The Teeth forced my hand."

I rushed him again, knowing there was nowhere to go.

He managed to dodge it, despite the small space filled with two grown men. "I'm not an abductor. I have much more important shit to do than take someone's daughter. But if I didn't do it, then my people were going to die."

This time, I slashed and slashed, kept going, not stopping until I finally drew some blood.

I got him on the arm, but it was barely a scratch.

Now he was against the bars, a little line of blood on his skin.

"They told me they wouldn't hurt her. Just use her as leverage. But when I dropped her off, they told me they were going to kill her…and I couldn't let that happen. That's why I brought her back."

"Interesting. Because my daughter told me you did it for a fucking boat." I lunged at him, ready to stab that blade right through his heart.

He pulled off another dodge. "And I lied."

I didn't care whether he lied or not. We weren't leaving this cell until he was a bloody corpse.

"Look, if I hadn't brought her back to you, she'd be dead right now."

"Motherfucker—" I came at him hard, swinging and swinging, missing my mark every time—until he knocked the blade from my hand and slid it out of the cell underneath the bars. I came at him with my fists instead, swinging and hitting him square in the jaw. When I hit him again, he blocked it. He blocked it again, protecting his face and his ribs. Around the cell, we moved, him blocking my strikes but never making any of his own.

"Stop hitting me, and I'll tell you everything. And I'll make you an offer you can't refuse."

All I wanted was him dead. It was all I could think about. I dropped my arms for a second to feign surrender, but then I rushed him and slammed his entire body against the wall. When he crumpled to the floor, I spat on him. "There's nothing you can do to barter for your life."

"Not even pledging an army of ten thousand powerful vampires to fight for you?"

I stopped in my tracks, the red haze of rage finally broken.

He looked up at me before he got to his feet, moving slowly as if that hit had winded him.

"*Vampires?*" It was a word I'd never heard.

He leaned against the wall and wiped the perspiration from his forehead. "I finally got your attention."

"I'm still going to kill you once we're done."

"Then you'll have no army."

"I'll kill you *after* the war has been won."

"You're one to hold a grudge, huh?"

"You think I won't snap your neck right now? Because I will, you pompous piece of shit." I shoved him hard in the shoulders, making him hit the wall again with a loud thud.

"We're distant relatives of the Teeth—*very distant*. We feed off human blood, but we don't kill our hosts… unless it's intentional. The vampires are at war with the Ethereal, elves that believe they're the true immortals and are intent on eradicating us from the planet. They spread a disease that's killed off most of the humans, so I sailed to these lands to get the antidote from the Teeth, because without humans to feed from, we'll eventually die. But they wouldn't give it to me unless I did this for them first. I'm sorry that I took your daughter, but believe me when I say no part of me wanted to do it."

I was at war with myself, wanting to kill him for what he'd done to Harlow, but also wanting to spare him because he could be the savior my people needed. Without knowing who my enemies were, I couldn't afford to turn away potential allies.

He watched me like he expected me to hit him again.

"They told me they wouldn't hurt her. But when I arrived, they said their plan had been exposed because you noticed my ship on the coast and you confronted them with their treason. They decided to make her write a letter and include a lock of her hair to draw you out, but she would be long dead before you even arrived."

I kept a straight face, but my breathing gave away my pain.

"I'm not going to lie to you and pretend I'm some hero with a strong moral compass, because I've done a lot of terrible shit that I'm unashamed to admit. But those weren't the terms of the deal, and I respect Harlow too much to let that happen to her. I fulfilled my requirement to the Teeth by delivering her—so my obligation was complete. I felt no guilt when I took her back, even if they are my cousins several times removed."

I was hooked on this story now, getting a much bigger and more detailed picture. A logical man would let bygones be bygones because of the context of this tale, but I wasn't a logical man when it came to my family—especially my daughter. I still wanted to kill him, and I would always want to kill him. "Who are their allies?"

"I don't know. They wouldn't share that with me. They just said they were a force to be reckoned with."

"Are they vampires?"

"No. If they were, he would have told me that."

"Then what lies to the east?"

"*I don't know,*" he snapped. "My land is far to the west."

"If your people are at war, how could they come to our aid?"

"I've been gone far longer than I anticipated, so that war has been won or lost by now."

"So you may not even have a home anymore?" I asked. "You may have nothing to offer me?"

He was quiet for a second, probably thinking about the friends and family he'd left behind. "I have faith that we won. The Ethereal are powerful beings—but the vampires are ruthless, and my brothers are vicious."

"Your brothers?"

"A lot of the specific details don't matter, but there are different factions of vampires, sired by different serpents. One brother is king of the Kingsnake Vampires and has one of our brothers as his general, and the other brother is king of the Cobra Vampires. And then my father is the first Original, so he's basically the king of them all."

"And what does that make you?"

"My father has selected me as his successor upon his unlikely death."

"Then you're a prince."

He gave a slight cringe. "If you must give it a title… then, yes."

"And you think you can convince them to vacate their lands after they've already fought in a war to aid strangers?" It seemed farfetched to me, and if I couldn't use him, then I could kill him now.

"My father is the first Original, the king of all vampires, and since I'm his favorite son, there's nothing he wouldn't do to spare my life. And my brothers would fight for me as well—even though we aren't always on the best terms."

I stared at him, finding an unlikely ally in my greatest enemy. "You're never allowed to leave my sight, so how will you call for aid?"

"I'll have to pen a letter, written in a way that will assure my father it's from me and not an impostor. Your couriers will have to follow my directions to sail to my lands, but to be honest, it's a far and arduous journey."

"My sailors can handle it."

"They may handle it better with my guidance—"

"Nice try." I moved to the bars and motioned to the guard to unlock the door.

"I'm a man of my word—"

"You are no man—as you just admitted."

"Whatever I may be, I keep my promises."

The guard opened the door, and I stepped out.

Aurelias tried to follow me, but I shut the door in his face and ordered the guard to lock it.

His eyes immediately soured. "I'll be dead by tomorrow if you don't release me. I feed on human blood, and it's been a very long time since my last feeding."

"And you think I'm going to let you feed on one of my citizens?"

His gaze hardened.

"No."

"I told you I would die—"

"There must be a compromise."

"I can sustain off animal blood—"

"Then I'll bring you several live animals."

"That will keep me alive, but I'll remain weak and emaciated—"

"*Good.*" I walked off, dismissing the prisoner. "I have no other use for you."

"If I have no ship, I have nowhere to run, so I'm not a threat to you or your people—"

"I will never grant you the opportunity to come near my daughter again, *vampire*. You used her enough, and I won't give you the chance to use her again—especially for her royal blood."

His arms rested on the rungs as he looked at me. "I would never do that."

"Because your honor means anything."

"I was starved on the journey home, but never once was I tempted. I didn't leave her side to feed on an animal because I feared for her safety more than my own lack of nourishment."

"My daughter can take care of herself."

"Not without a sword, which she didn't have—"

"I will spare your life, but I will not grant you freedom. You will send for your kin to fight for us, and the war will happen while you're trapped in this dungeon. Once the war is over and we're victorious, you may leave with your people." I turned and walked off again, finished with this nuisance.

"Harlow will vouch for my character—if you ask her."

I stopped again and slowly turned to face him. "I'm sure the woman who threw you in here has nothing but nice things to say about you." I was proud my daughter was smart enough to manipulate this asshole and lock him up under the castle she slept in every night. She didn't feel indebted to him for rescuing her, not when he'd abducted her in the first place. She had a good head on her shoulders—and she would make a brilliant queen one day.

"Ask her."

I walked off.

"*Ask her.*"

23

HARLOW

Once my father returned to the room, I broke free of my brother's hold and rushed to him. "I told him I wouldn't kill him—"

"And I didn't."

My face was probably red and puffy from resisting my brother the last few minutes, and I was sure I still looked pissed off, even though I'd gotten the outcome I wanted. It took me a second to withdraw my rage. "What happened?"

"He's a vampire." He walked past me and returned to his seat at the head of the table. "Distant relations of the Teeth, beings that feed on the blood of humans."

I watched him sit down, and I took a moment to process what he said.

His arm rested across the table, and his fingers curled up against his lip as he became lost in thought.

We returned to our seats at the table, and I thought about what Aurelias had said to me, that if he remained locked in that cage, he would die. Because he couldn't eat the food the guards served—only the blood in their veins. A shiver ran down my spine, because I realized I'd been alone with a monster on several occasions, had slept beside him, completely vulnerable to his bite.

My father continued. "I spared his life because he offered his people in the upcoming war. He'll write a letter, and our sailors will deliver it to their domain, requesting their assistance in this battle. In exchange, I'll release him when the battle is over."

Atticus digested the information in silence. "A vampire...I've never heard of such a thing."

"Nor have I," my mother said. "The world is bigger than we know."

I was stunned into silence, feeling like a bigger fool for having such a heated affair with him. He wasn't even human, and I'd had no idea. "He'll die if he doesn't feed, so we can't leave him down there."

"He said he can sustain off animal blood," my father said. "So that's what I offered for the duration of his stay. Without knowing the identity of our enemies, I can't afford to turn away allies. If vampires are anything like the Teeth, they're powerful. And in my interaction with him, he had the kind of speed and agility I've never seen before. He seemed to predict my moves before I even made them."

"Then is inviting them to our lands a good idea?" Mother asked. "An invitation to a superior race may not be the best idea. If they're that fast and powerful, they could simply dominate our people and take the throne."

My father always thought of everything before anyone else did. "He may be more powerful than most men, but he's not more powerful than a dragon."

Mother stared at him, her eyes full of unspoken words. "Perhaps we should have this conversation in private, Huntley."

He held her gaze, a mountain at the head of the table, his stare fierce. "Harlow will succeed you as queen someday. She's an adult now, and we're on the brink of war—and I think it's vital she learns from this experience." He exercised restraint as he spoke, like he dreaded every word that came out of his mouth. The conclusion of his words was accompanied by a sigh—a painful one. He turned to look at me, his eyes guarded and agonized. "I'm proud of you for the way you handled our prisoner. You could have felt indebted to him for rescuing you, but you were smart enough to understand he was your enemy the moment he took you. If that monster were free, he would be killing other innocent people, just like the man he killed when he occupied his home."

I swallowed, realizing that the home he'd pretended was his had belonged to someone else, a citizen of Delacroix.

"You have a good head on your shoulders, Harlow."

I didn't tell him the truth, that I'd thrown Aurelias in the dungeon out of pettiness, that I was hurt by the way he'd fooled me, dangled a piece of candy in front of me that I could never have. It wasn't strategic whatsoever, but like the coward I was, I said nothing.

My father continued. "Aurelias will write the letter. I'll send a letter to Ian to inform him of current events.

We should send scouts next, to learn whatever we possibly can about our neighbors to the east."

"Will you return to HeartHolme?" Mother asked.

"Not right now." He turned to meet her look. "I'm not prepared to leave my family again so soon."

I made my way to the dungeon beneath the castle, passing the guard at the entryway and entering the prison with no windows. The chandelier and sconces provided low light, the kind of light that made you sleepy all the time. In the summertime, it was nice and cold, but in the winter, it could be chilly and intolerable.

Aurelias sat on the floor and leaned against the wall, his ankles crossed with his arms folded in front of his body. He looked a lot better compared to the last time I saw him, so he must have fed on the animal blood the guards provided. He sat, eyes hostile and accusatory.

"*You're mad at me?*" I asked incredulously. "You're alive, aren't you?"

"I may as well be dead." He looked away, staring at a different section of the cell like I wasn't standing at the bars.

"You're being dramatic."

His head snapped back to me. "Your father sentenced me to remain imprisoned until the war is over. That could take months—assuming you even win."

"I think most people would be relieved they're spared from battle."

"I belong on the battlefield, not trapped beneath ground like a criminal."

"You *are* a criminal—"

"I told you my tale, and I did exactly what anyone else would have done in my situation. Harlow, you're too damn smart to be this petty."

"You killed an innocent man and invaded his home. That's murder."

He rolled his eyes. "Look—"

"Asshole."

"I offered him money to leave, but he refused. He didn't leave me a choice."

"Not killing someone is always a choice."

He got to his feet and approached the bars. "*Princess*, you've never had to survive on your own, so don't stand there and judge me for actions you would take yourself. And if you deny it, then that just means you lack the experience to know what the real world is like. We both know you didn't lock me up down here because I killed some guy nobody even noticed was gone—"

"You're a dick."

His arms slid through the bars. "You locked me up down here because I embarrassed you."

"And you would kill me if the situations were reversed."

"I'm not sure where I earned this reputation as a ruthless killer, considering everything I did for you." His eyes burned into mine. "I never tried to feed from you. You have no idea how hungry I was, but the thought didn't cross my mind. I could have bled you out and found another way home—but I didn't. I get you're still angry at me, but don't destroy my reputation when I don't deserve it. There's no reason to keep me locked down here, not if I'm officially your ally."

"My father doesn't want you near me."

"If I didn't feed then, why would I feed now?" His eyes bored into mine with ferocity. "I keep my word. I won't harm your citizens, I'll feed on animal blood, and I'll help you face whatever you're up against. I'm not staying down here until my people arrive."

"Well, you don't have much of a choice."

His eyes stilled as he took in my face. "You're just like your father."

"I take that as a compliment."

"He arrogantly came in here without his armor, and I could have hurt him pretty badly if I'd wanted to, even in my weakened state. But I didn't. I took a beating like a dog to prove, for the millionth time, that I'm not a threat to you."

My eyes shifted away, uncomfortable that my father had exposed himself like that.

"Harlow."

My eyes remained fixed for a moment before I looked at him again.

"Tell your father to release me. I may not have earned his trust—but I've earned yours."

I looked away again.

"You know I have."

"My father…is not someone who can be reasoned with."

"Unless you're the one doing the reasoning."

I pulled out the parchment and the quill and ink. "Write your letter and provide directions to the sailors."

His eyes remained on me. "Everything that happened between us was real. If you think I fucked you like that and it was all pretend…you're crazy."

"Write the letter."

"It was so real that I turned on my allies and saved you."

"Shut up and write the damn letter—"

"*Harlow.*"

I continued to hold the parchment through the bars, standing so close to him that it was like the bars weren't there. "I really liked you…" I dropped my chin, embarrassed that I'd said that out loud.

He didn't say anything, just stared at me.

Now I regretted speaking those words, putting the truth out there for him to hear.

"I wouldn't have saved you if the feeling weren't mutual."

I kept my eyes down, too ashamed to meet his look.

"You're the only person who can convince your father to let me go—and you know it's the right thing to do."

I kept my eyes on the parchment paper in my hands.

"Please…"

His tone made me look up again.

"I promise I won't flee. I promise I won't feed on your people. I promise to fulfill my pledge and help you win this war in exchange for my freedom. You've seen my character and can attest to it. I need you to do that now—because I would rather die than be locked up in here."

24

IVORY

I was in bed reading when Huntley walked inside.

He'd been in his study all night, quiet and contemplative, wearing a hard expression that suggested he didn't want to be bothered. He walked in, set his weapons against the door like always, and then stripped off each piece of his battle armor before removing the uniform underneath.

I knew our time of peace was over when Huntley wore his armor around the castle, prepared for an attack that could come at any moment. He undressed fully, even removing his boxers, and his dick was rock hard.

His eyes moved to mine, demanding and even a little angry, so I knew what would come next.

I barely had a chance to set my book on the nightstand before he grabbed me by the ankles and dragged me to him. He yanked off my underwear, folded me at the edge of the bed, and then pushed himself inside me without even waiting for me to be ready.

I gasped in both pain and pleasure.

Then he grabbed me by the throat and squeezed me so hard I could barely breathe.

He fucked me like that, standing at the edge of the bed, thrusting so hard the headboard tapped against the wall and was probably audible to the guards at their posts outside.

I lay there and enjoyed it, feeling like a woman in her youth rather than a woman he had fucked for decades.

I was about to fall asleep when he was on top of me again. He grabbed my legs and folded me underneath him before he entered again, this time slow and steady, his lips finding mine and kissing me.

When we were young, several rounds were normal, but as we got older, that became uncommon. But he was on me after a short break, like he'd been gone for months rather than a few days.

"What's gotten into you?" My nails sliced into his muscular back, feeling the powerful muscles shift and move under my touch.

"You're mine." He continued to rock into me, making love to me rather than fucking me the way he did before. "That's what."

He washed off in the shower after we were done.

It was late, far later than we usually went to bed, but now I was wide awake.

He returned to the bedroom in a new pair of boxers, his hair slightly wet, drops still on his shoulders. He was a mountain of muscle, a powerhouse of strength, having the weight of an ox. He pulled back the sheets and got into bed without offering an explanation.

"Huntley?"

He lay there, one arm tucked under his head, his other arm on his chest. "What is it, baby?"

"Did something happen?"

He was quiet.

"While you were in HeartHolme?" When men were riddled with guilt after cheating, they brought flowers and gifts. They were suddenly warm and affectionate, realizing what they'd just gambled. I knew that wasn't the case with Huntley—but something had happened.

"Ian and Avice have separated."

I couldn't contain my gasp. "*What*? Since when?"

"A couple months now."

"I don't understand... What happened?"

Huntley propped himself on the pillows next to me, looking across the bedroom. He told me the entire tale.

"Ian..."

"I was disappointed in him too, but she's not innocent in this either."

"He must be devastated."

"He is," he said quietly. "I tried to talk to her...but accomplished nothing."

"I'll speak to her when I have a chance."

"I think that's a good idea."

I sank into the pillows, still in disbelief. "Avice should be working to repair the relationship with Ian and Lila. I'm disappointed in her for allowing this estrangement to continue."

"I don't have all the details on that. For all we know, she's spoken to Lila."

They were the kind of couple that I assumed would last forever. Knowing their marriage was over was as painful as the idea of my marriage being over.

"If I lost you…" Huntley continued his stare across the room. "I'd be in worse shape than him."

My eyes softened as I stared at the side of his face, unsure what I'd done to earn the unflinching loyalty of a man who only got sexier as he aged. He could have replaced me with a woman half his age who was just as in love with him, but he continued to look at me like I was the only woman he desired.

I moved into his side and used his hard chest as a pillow.

His thick arm wrapped around me and brought me close, his lips brushing a kiss to my temple. "I love you, baby."

Puffy, white clouds formed in my chest, and birds sang in my ears. "I love you too."

25

HUNTLEY

I sat behind my desk and stared while Ivory spoke.

"I've sent letters to the stewards, telling them to prepare the armies for battle and asking them to travel to Delacroix so we can have an in-person discussion about current events. I think for something this important, sending letters back and forth doesn't make sense."

I listened to every word, but a part of me was distracted by the tightness of her figure in her uniform. I liked it when she wore dresses, because it was easy to pull up the material and fuck her on my desk, but nothing turned me on more than seeing her in a uniform identical to mine, her trousers tight on her toned legs, her tits full in the slender clothing, her sword at her hip, her bow and arrows across her back, a little dagger on the opposite hip.

Her eyes narrowed when she finished speaking, like she suspected I hadn't been listening.

"I agree."

Her eyes remained narrowed before a soft smile moved on to her lips. "You weren't listening, were you?"

"Baby, I always listen to you."

"Sure..."

She turned around and walked off.

My eyes stared at her ass until she was gone.

A moment later, Harlow walked inside, wearing a long floral dress with her hair in a tight braid. "Father, may I speak to you?"

Ivory was gone from my mind quicker than a blown-out candle. "Of course, sweetheart." I leaned back in the chair, still surprised that Harlow was a perfect blend of her mother and me, that she and Atticus were my proudest legacy.

Instead of firing off right from the beginning, speaking her mind at a million miles an hour as usual, she was quiet. She sat down, crossed her legs, and looked off into space for a while.

My eyes narrowed. "Everything alright?"

"Yes," she said quickly. "Everything is fine."

Then why didn't it seem fine?

Her gaze finally found mine, now with a shine of strength. "I wanted to talk about Aurelias."

"What about him?"

There was another bout of hesitation. "I think we should release him."

"Why?" My unconditional love for my daughter always provided me an indescribable warmth in my chest, but that intoxicating joy was snuffed out the second she said those words to me. "He deserves the edge of my blade, not freedom."

"I never said freedom. But I don't think it's necessary to put him in a cage."

"You're the one who put him there in the first place."

"Because I was angry—"

"And what's changed?" Now I wanted to march down there and swipe his head clean from his shoulders for manipulating my daughter.

"My conscience."

"Your conscience." I said the words slowly because they were sour on my tongue. "Harlow, he kidnapped you—"

"*Father*." She held up her hand to silence me, knowing a tirade of screams would reverberate against the walls if she didn't. "He explained everything to us, and if the situations were reversed, I think you would kidnap some girl to save your people, your wife, your kids…"

"He doesn't have a wife and kids—"

"Doesn't mean he doesn't have someone worth dying for," she said calmly. "Look me in the eye and tell me you wouldn't do the same."

I held her gaze, my temples pounding with ferocity.

"I know you," she said softly. "There's nothing you wouldn't do for your people and for your family. Nothing at all."

My eyes shifted away. I would never hurt an innocent woman, take her away from her loving home, not as a father who understood how it felt to have a daughter. But if it was her life or my daughter's…I'd kill her myself.

"He said he forfeited his deal with the Teeth when he knew what they would do to me…and I believe him."

"Why?"

"Because I know him…in a way."

That wasn't good enough for me.

"It's hard to explain."

I simmered in silence, disappointed my daughter's head was turned so easily.

"He showed his true character when he saved me. That's much more important than when he had no choice but to take me."

"Harlow, you're too smart to let this man manipulate you."

"He didn't manipulate me—"

"Your change of heart says otherwise. You put him down there for a reason."

"Because I was mad—"

"And you should still be mad."

"But I was mad for the wrong reasons."

"Wrong reasons?" I asked.

She looked away, her fingers fidgeting with her dress. "It's complicated."

"Nothing is too complicated for me to understand."

Her gaze remained elsewhere. "Father...this is more of Mother's territory."

A flash of anger ran through me, followed by the kind of discomfort that made me sick. I didn't even entertain the meaning of her words, shutting them off so tightly that a single thought couldn't slip through. "You're blind, Harlow."

"You're the one who can't see straight when it comes to me."

Ferocity burned inside me like blazing-hot flames.

"When we fled the Teeth, he took care of me. He gave me his cloak. He made me a fire so I wouldn't freeze to death—even though it could have drawn yetis to us and gotten him killed. He could have fed on me as he starved, but he never touched me. Yes, he took me...

but he's done a lot more than that. Because of him, we'll have an army that our enemy doesn't expect."

"Only to save his life."

"He's still an ally. And I think we should treat him as an ally rather than a prisoner."

All I could do was stare at her, my anger thriving unregulated inside my muscles and veins. The fact that he'd had an intimate relationship with my daughter made me hate him even more. "No."

"Father—"

"That's my final answer." I gave her an ice-cold stare, telling her not to push this, not when I was this pissed off. There was nothing I wouldn't give my daughter, so she wasn't used to hearing me say the word no, but I wouldn't give in. "I'll release him once he makes good on his promise."

"Father—"

"You're dismissed."

"*I'm dismissed*?" She said each word slowly, her head cocked and her eyes pained. "I've always admired you as a king because you're kind and just, but ruthless when necessary. But this isn't fair. This is—"

"You're not going to get your way. Now, get out of my office."

She flinched like I'd just slapped her. Her eyes clouded with hurt, and her nostrils flared like an angry animal about to strike. But then she left her chair and walked out, not saying another word.

I'd never spoken to my daughter that way, and I was too angry to feel bad about it. But I knew I would feel differently about that in a couple of hours.

26

IVORY

I was in the aviary, sitting at the desk and rolling up my letter to slip it into the weightless tube. I would attach it to the peregrine falcon, the fastest bird on the planet, and get it to the steward as quickly as possible.

Harlow appeared at the top of the stairs, not winded from the long staircase, but beet red with anger. "I need to talk to you."

I closed the tube and twisted it tight. "What did Atticus do now?"

"Not him." She dropped down into the chair across from me. "Father."

"Oh. I'm still used to the two of you fighting like cats and dogs." I set aside the tube and gave my daughter my full attention. "What did your father do? The two of you are usually two peas in a pod."

"I thought that same thing."

"What happened?"

"I asked him to release Aurelias, and to be frank, he was a dick about it."

"Refusing to release the prisoner who abducted you doesn't exactly make him a dick."

"I made my case, and he refuses to listen because he's too stubborn."

"You're also stubborn."

Harlow's eyes narrowed. "Why are you taking his side?"

"I'm not taking anyone's side, Harlow. I just find it hard to believe your father was a dick, especially to you."

Harlow told me everything Aurelias had done for her, that he was trustworthy and deserved to live outside that metal cage. "I only put him in there because he hurt my pride, and that was wrong of me. But I'm petty like my father…and stubborn, apparently."

I gave her a small smile.

"Now Father is doing the same thing. He knows I'm right, but he refuses to listen."

"I think he refuses to grant mercy to a man who hurt his daughter."

"He didn't really hurt me…just disappointed me." Her eyes traveled somewhere else, and so did her mind.

"How did he disappoint you?"

She continued to look away. "I liked him hard, and I liked him fast…"

"Do you still like him?"

"No." Her eyes found mine again.

"Are you sure?" I asked. "Why else are you pleading for his release?"

"Because I need to be objective and put aside my personal feelings for the good of our Kingdoms. Aurelias is smart and powerful, and if he has allies who are just like him, that's exactly what we need. And I shouldn't take his deceit so personally anyway. If it were someone else, I wouldn't have cared."

"Meaning?"

Her eyes avoided mine. "Like I said…I liked him hard, and I liked him fast."

I watched my daughter turn quiet and contemplative, watched the way the heaviness flashed across her eyes like it never had before. When she'd told me about other guys she'd been with, it was always fun and adventurous, nothing with any real feelings. She just enjoyed being young and beautiful. But now, it was different. It was the first time she'd admitted that fun and adventurous wasn't enough for her. "I'll speak to your father."

Her eyes found mine again. "You will?"

"He's very protective of you—and I think he's taken that too far."

"Like I've told Ethan and others, it's not my fault they hoped for something more. Now I'm on the other end of that…and I need to stop being a sore loser. I need to buck up and take rejection in stride."

"It doesn't sound like he ever rejected you. And what is it about him that sets him apart from the others? Like Ethan."

"Well…you've seen him." She released a chuckle.

I smiled. "Not my type…but I see what you mean."

"He hasn't bathed and is trapped in a cell, and he's still the most gorgeous guy I've ever seen."

"If it's only looks, it probably would have burned out pretty quickly."

"Maybe. But I liked him for him too."

"You hardly know him."

"But I know the things that matter. That he has a heart, even though he wishes he didn't. That he doesn't wear his heart on his sleeve because he safeguards it like treasure. He acts like a dick, but he's noble at his core. When Father attacked him in his cell, he didn't fight back, even though he could have. I've seen him in action and know what he's capable of. He didn't have to respect Father like that—but he did."

"It sounds like he likes you too."

After a long pause, she spoke. "Maybe. But that doesn't matter anymore…"

27

HUNTLEY

I had dinner in my study and didn't speak to anyone for the rest of the day. I was tempted to sleep on the couch, because I knew what was waiting for me in my bedchambers. Harlow would have run to Ivory next, and I knew my wife would give me her opinion on the matter.

An opinion I didn't ask for.

Late that evening, the door to my study opened, and Ivory entered in her pajamas, one of my shirts that fit her like a dress. With her arms crossed over her chest, she approached the desk, that potent look in her eye.

I held her stare, prepared for all the shit she had to say.

"Huntley."

I looked away, already wounded by the sound of my own name.

"You're entitled to your anger, but as King of Delacroix, you have to be objective rather than petty. You have to listen to reason rather than anger—"

"I don't feel like listening to this right now."

"Too bad, Huntley." She came closer to the desk, her eyes bright in disappointment.

"I'm King of Delacroix, King of Kingdoms, and I can do whatever I want—"

"And I'm Queen of Kingdoms, and I have a say whether you like it or not."

Normally, I'd get hard at a conversation like this, but not this one. "He took our daughter from us. She could have been injured, killed, something even worse…and you're prepared to let that go?"

"I think our daughter makes a sound argument for his release."

"He's a blood-sucking vampire."

"Who has complete control of his hunger. Otherwise, he would have fed on Harlow when there was nothing to stop him."

"I don't like him."

"She's not asking you to like him."

"She's asking me to trust him. I know he hurt my daughter in more ways than one, and he's a damn idiot for thinking I would ever stop punishing him for that." I got to my feet. "I will make every day of his life as insufferable as possible until he's gone. I will make him wish he were dead before he leaves these shores. Motherfucker thought he could screw around with my daughter and get away with it—"

"Huntley."

I snapped and slammed my hand down on the desk, making my glass fall to the floor and shatter. "I should march down there right now and kill him like he deserved in the first place."

"*Huntley.*"

I avoided her gaze, looked into the cold fire where flames would be in the winter.

"Harlow is a young woman who will get her heart broken a few times before she finds the right man. It's life. There's nothing you or I can do to prevent it. Even the King of Kingdoms isn't powerful enough to prevent heartache."

"But I can kill them..."

She watched me, pity growing in her eyes. "Huntley, you know I'm right. You know Harlow is right."

I avoided her gaze out of pure stubbornness.

"You said you trust your daughter's instinct. Now's the time to prove it."

I ignored her.

"Huntley—"

"I'll consider your request. That's the most I can offer you."

Ivory stopped her crusade and turned quiet.

I waited for her to leave so I could wallow in my quiet rage.

"Thank you."

I continued to wait for her to leave, but she stayed put.

"Yes?"

"It's late."

"I'll sleep on the couch."

"No, you're coming to bed."

I turned to look at her.

"And if you don't, I'll make you." Her eyes burned with the fire of a queen who commanded respect from everyone who looked at her. She didn't carry weapons or armor, but she was still terrifying…and beautiful.

28

AURELIAS

I tried to be diplomatic about the situation, but if I didn't get what I wanted, I would grab the guard who brought the tray of food I only ate so the food would keep coming. And once the guard with the keys ran over, I would kill them both and walk out of there.

But I preferred to be let out, so I continued to be patient.

Without lifting my gaze, I knew Harlow had entered the dungeon because I could feel her mind. I could only feel heightened emotions, but I'd become so acquainted with her mind that I could recognize it as a unique signature. It was no different from spotting an acquaintance on the street, except I didn't need sight to recognize her.

I lifted my chin and watched her approach the bars, wearing a white floral dress with her dark hair in a tight braid. A tightness seized my chest as I looked at her, a desire so distinct it made my mouth go dry. Her beauty endured on our arduous journey, but now it shone like a white candle in the dark. My eyes remained hard and feigned indifference, but my skin prickled as flashbacks moved across my mind.

"I talked to my father." Her arms slid through the bars and rested on the metal, exposing herself to my grasp. I could threaten to break her arm unless they unlocked the door, and as much as I wanted to be free, I wanted to hurt her even less. "I'm sorry."

I pushed off the wall and approached, my arms sliding through the bars on the outside of hers, our faces close together. "I've never encountered anyone who's wanted me dead more, so I'm not surprised." Our faces were so near each other, but separated by the iron bars that my strength couldn't demolish.

"I've asked my mother to speak to him," she said. "Perhaps she can change his mind."

I released a quiet snort.

"What?"

"Your mother probably hates me more."

"My mother is actually the more pragmatic one of the two. When my father's mind is clouded with anger, he can't see the tip of his nose on his own face."

"Maybe in most circumstances, but a loving mother can easily turn into a mama bear."

"She is a mama bear, but she sees a lot of herself in me, so she gives me more space to learn and grow. My father has a harder time with it. He tries to respect me as an adult, but his protective side has the ferocity of a dragon."

"Yes, I've noticed."

She smiled. "Maybe he'll come around."

"Maybe." I wouldn't hold my breath.

I expected her to leave now that the news had been relayed, but she remained. "Why didn't you…bite me?"

I stared at her fair skin, the subtle tones of pink in her cheeks, the sparkle of light in her sky-blue eyes.

"You were starving…"

"That would have required me to explain what I am."

"You said it to my father freely."

"No, I did it to barter for my life," I said. "He would have killed me otherwise. And even if I did ask, you would have said no—as you should."

"So…you always ask permission first? Because the Teeth don't."

"I prefer consent, yes."

"And why would anyone consent?"

My eyes narrowed. "You're asking a lot of questions."

"I've never met a vampire before. Never even heard of one until now."

"Well…when a vampire feeds, it's more than just a feeding. It's an intimate experience."

"Intimate, how?"

"Erotic."

Her eyes shifted back and forth between mine, and I imagined she had flashbacks of the two of us together, fucking like animals on the couch in the living room. "So…it leads to sex."

"It goes hand in hand."

"I don't think blood and sex go together."

"It's one of those things that doesn't make sense unless you've experienced it."

She continued to stare at me.

"The fangs of a vampire release a flood of chemicals that elicit pleasure. So, when I bite my lover, she becomes drunk on the chemicals, and then she becomes drunk on my dick too. It's borderline hallucinogenic."

Fire burned from her core, the flames white-hot in the center, the warmth radiating from her like a beacon of light in winter. There was a shiver too, a streak of ice right in the center. Her eyes shifted away, like my words bored her, but her insides told a different story.

I felt my skin prickle again, but once I put up that wall, the surge of desire I had dissipated like steam on the wind. "We're related to the Teeth, but we're nothing like them. They're bloodthirsty creatures, intent on feeding on more than blood, like muscle and bone. Vampires can be peaceful—if we choose."

"And are you peaceful?" she asked quietly.

I inhaled a slow breath as I considered the answer. "It depends on the vampire. My brother is the king of Kingsnake Vampires, and he's always been adamant about maintaining a peaceful balance with the humans. But one of my other brothers King Cobra feels much differently, sees humans as livestock for us to shepherd."

"And you?"

"I'm an Original."

"And are you peaceful?"

The Originals were the most violent of all. "I think that's enough questions for the day."

Her eyes flashed in disappointment. "You have more important matters to attend to?"

"If I tell you everything about my kind, there's no incentive to free me." I pulled my arms from the bars and retreated to the wall where I spent all my time, wondering if my father would launch a thousand ships to come to my rescue if I didn't return soon.

She stayed at the bars and continued to stare at me. "I've always had an incentive to free you."

It was hard to know how much time had passed since Kingsnake and Larisa had left me here. It was months, but how many months, I wasn't sure. I'd been in Delacroix awhile before I made my move on Harlow, learning about the city and the royals who ruled over it. If my family was victorious in the war against the Ethereal, I knew they would sail here to rescue me.

But the Teeth had abandoned their stronghold, so Kingsnake wouldn't be able to question them. He knew I'd traveled to Delacroix to kidnap their princess, and that would probably be his next move. But I wasn't sure how he would figure out I was trapped beneath the castle.

I'd have to break out of here myself if King Rolfe didn't change his mind.

At that moment, heavy boots sounded on the stairs, and then the King of Delacroix appeared, dressed in his armor and uniform, his two-handed heavy sword across his back along with his axe—a peculiar choice for a weapon.

I remained on the floor, my forearm propped on my bent knee, wondering if he'd come down to void our agreement and kill me instead.

He stood at the bars and stared at me, looking like a pissed-off grizzly bear whose cub I had mishandled. He was a few years younger than my father appeared, the age at which he was turned, but he clearly didn't sit on a throne and order others to do his bidding. He was muscular like an ox, his neck so tight the cords looked like rivers that led to an ocean underneath his clothing. There was some gray in his hair, but not much. He would be an admirable opponent on the battlefield, and I respected him for that.

He was also stubborn like my father and refused to speak first. He continued his angry stare.

I got to my feet and approached the bars, ready to speak to him face-to-face, to accept the sentence that I would somehow escape. Taking my life after I'd spared Harlow's was a shitty way to show his gratitude, and I wouldn't accept my death as punishment. If I had to kill him to escape, then so be it.

King Rolfe continued to stare.

I stared back.

Slowly, his eyebrows rose up his face, and that cold fury heightened.

Neither one of us was willing to cave first.

He started to turn away.

I had to take the hit. "Are you here to kill me or release me?"

He stilled at my words then slowly turned back to look at me through the iron bars. "Unlock the door."

That still didn't answer my question.

The guard came over with the key and unlocked the door.

King Rolfe opened it, a barrier no longer between us.

I stayed inside the cage, suspecting it was a trap.

"You asked my daughter to free you, didn't you?"

Yes, it was definitely a trap. I stepped out of the cage, and the second I was free, he slammed the door shut.

His big hand grabbed my neck and smashed me into the iron bars.

I knew it was coming, but I chose not to block it, to let him think he had the upper hand.

He pinned me in place, glaring at me with blue eyes identical to Harlow's. "These are the conditions of your release." His fingers remained hard on my neck, cutting off most of my air supply when I didn't need air to stay alive. The act of breathing was just a habit that couldn't be broken. "Run—and I'll kill you."

I had nowhere to go, not without a ship.

"Feed on anyone—and I'll kill you."

Since bloodletting wasn't a part of their culture, it would be hard to come across the offer anyway.

"Come anywhere near my daughter—and I'll kill you."

I'd anticipated that one.

"Do we understand each other?"

I nodded.

"I asked you a question, asshole."

I was used to being at the top of the food chain, the second-in-command of all vampires, and now I was on the bottom rung of social status. It didn't feel good, and it provoked my ego. "Yes."

He slammed me against the bars again before he let me go. "You'll reside in the cottage that you stole, guards stationed outside your residence at all times. Fuck with me—and you're dead."

"The threats are unnecessary when I've agreed to be your ally."

His eyes narrowed. "You know we'll never be allies—not after what you did."

"With all due respect, your daughter is fine."

He moved into me and shoved me against the bars again. "But I'm not. If you live long enough to be a father someday, you'll understand the mercy I've shown you. You'll understand the unbelievable strength I've displayed."

I would never be a father. That privilege had been taken from me—not that I'd wanted it anyway. "I betrayed an ally to spare your daughter's life, so it's clear I hold no ill will toward you or your people."

"But I will always hold ill will toward you, *vampire*."

Find out what happens next in **The Broken Prince**, Book 5 in the Dirty Blood series.

Printed in Great Britain
by Amazon